"You're trembling," he whispered.

"Tell me something I don't know."

"Okay." He leaned in closer to her ear, and the faint scent of her shampoo had him trembling himself. "I'm falling in love with you."

She jerked her head up to stare at him and her eyes widened, just as the front door opened.

CHRISTINE LYNXWILER and her husband, Kevin, live in the foothills of the beautiful Ozark Mountains in their home state of Arkansas. Christine's greatest earthly joy is her family and aside from God's work, spending time with them is her top priority. To fulfill her desire to help other writers, she currently serves as the president of American Christian Romance Writers, an international writing organization with over 300 members.

HEARTSONG PRESENTS

Books by Christine Lynxwiler
HP526—In Search of Love

Patchwork and Politics

Christine Lynxwiler

Heartsong Presents

Dedicated to the brave men and women—past, present, and future—who fight to keep our country free, as well as the legislators who selflessly work to ensure each citizen enjoys that freedom. And most of all, to the One who died on the cross so that all who follow Him can have eternal liberty.

Special thanks to Jana Nichols of *Quilts By Jana* for letting me pick her brain and Arkansas State Senator Tim Wooldridge for filling me in on the world of politics. Any errors are mine alone, made in spite of their wonderful expert advice. As always, thanks to my beloved Kevin and our girls for their love and patience.

A note from the Author:
I love to hear from my readers! You may correspond with me by writing:

Christine Lynxwiler
Author Relations
PO Box 719
Uhrichsville, OH 44683

ISBN 1-58660-860-6

PATCHWORK AND POLITICS

All scripture quotations, unless otherwise indicated, are taken from the HOLY BIBLE, NEW INTERNATIONAL VERSION®. NIV®. Copyright © 1973, 1978, 1984 by International Bible Society. Used by permission of Zondervan Publishing House. All rights reserved.

All of the characters and events in this book are fictitious. Any resemblance to actual persons, living or dead, or to actual events is purely coincidental.

PRINTED IN THE U.S.A.

prologue

"This can't be!" Megan Watson slammed the newspaper on the dining room table. How could someone she had once welcomed into her home, someone she'd trusted, turn out to be so evil?

Twenty-three-month-old Sarah awakened at the sudden outcry from her mother and began to wail. Still trembling, Megan stepped to the playpen and lifted the sleepy toddler to her shoulder. As she jostled Sarah gently, her gaze fell again on the blaring caption. Still reeling from the unexpected attack, she fought the desire to collapse on the floor and join the baby's cries.

Instead, determined to think rationally, she retrieved the star-spangled newspaper from the table. This edition featured Fourth of July advertisements from a variety of businesses. The accusing headline seemed out of place.

GRIEF-STRICKEN WIDOW OR GUILTY CO-CONSPIRATOR?

Her image stared back at her from above the hateful words. She was dressed in black, tears streaming down her face. A close look at the background revealed the photo had been taken two months ago as she left the cemetery after Barry's funeral.

Her hands shook as she scanned the article that debated her guilt in her late husband's investment disaster. Right next to the piece about her, a furniture store ad proclaimed, "Let Freedom Ring!" Megan shook her head. What about her freedom? What about the right to be considered innocent until proven guilty?

Immediately following Barry's death, shock and anger had rippled through the community when long-time friends discovered their investments in his theme park venture were lost. Megan understood their despair. She should. She'd been taken in by Barry Watson's charm as well. And even though she would do anything to make up their financial loss, there were some things worse than losing money. Like betrayal by someone you love.

She snuggled the sleeping Sarah closer and moved a pile of boxes over so she could sink into the wicker rocker. The top box was marked "Sarah's room." A white eyelet quilt peeked out from under the lid. Her grandmother had made it as soon as she'd found out Megan was pregnant.

Although losing her precious grandmother had been a nightmare, at least Granny Lola wasn't here to see her now. She'd always been sure Megan would make something of herself one day.

Megan bit back a half-sob, half-laugh as she considered the boxes that constituted her life. She'd sold everything of value, so there wasn't much left to look at. A man was coming this afternoon to pick up the rest of the furniture.

She ran her hand across the smooth arm of the rocker. Barry had bought it for her for ten dollars at a yard sale when she was pregnant with Sarah. She'd considered saving it, but there were rocking chairs at the farm. Her past wasn't worth holding on to.

The jangling of the phone interrupted her maudlin thoughts. During the first few weeks after news of Barry's death and financial ruin had become public, she had let the machine take the calls. Now, since she'd developed a plan of sorts, she answered them all, preferring to face her troubles head on.

"Hello?"

"Megan Watson?" The raspy voice sounded odd, as if the speaker couldn't draw a deep breath.

"Yes?"

"Who's going to take care of all the old people you've swindled?"

"Who is this?"

"Who are you? People trusted you. How can you live with what you did?"

"I didn't—"

"Save your excuses for the police."

The line went dead. Megan sat with the phone still in her hand. "If you'd like to make a call, please hang up and—" Careful not to wake Sarah, she quickly pushed the off button.

Her heart thudded in her chest. The caller had sounded like a man, but he'd definitely been disguising his voice. Judging from the article she'd just read, Ivo Pletka seemed the most likely suspect. The reporter had been Barry's best friend through high school and college. But she hadn't heard from him since the funeral.

He'd once been a frequent guest in their home, bragging on Megan's cooking and teasing her about making him want to get married. Now he was persecuting her in the statewide newspaper, trying to make her look like the mastermind behind Barry's fraud. When had the world turned upside down? How could she ever trust anyone again?

Given the circumstances, Megan could accept Ivo's anger. His grandfather was a Russian immigrant who hadn't lived far from her grandmother. The elderly man had lost money in Barry's deal. A month or so ago, Megan heard that his wife had admitted him to a nursing home. Megan's heart had ached for the cheerful old man and his beloved grandson. But she still wished Ivo had come to her and checked out the facts for himself.

In a way, she hoped the anonymous caller had been Ivo. Better to have one known enemy than many unknown ones.

The phone rang again. Anger poured over Megan, white and hot, jolting the fear from her body. She yanked up the receiver. "Hello," she snapped.

"Hi, Honey." Her mother's troubled voice sent shards of guilt through her. She'd obviously seen the newspaper.

"Hi, Mom." She should have made an exception this afternoon and let the machine answer.

"How are you doing?"

"I'm okay. How are you?"

"We're fine. I was wondering if this might be a good time for me to come up and help you. . .with the baby and all. . ." Her mother's voice drifted off as if she didn't know what to say.

"Not really." Tears threatened to clog Megan's voice completely. She cleared her throat. "I appreciate it, though."

"Oh. I'd like to help. Like I told you—"

"I know you would, Mom." Each word had to squeeze past a lump the size of Texas. If her mother realized she was crying, she wouldn't let it go. "There's not really anything you can do right now. But thanks."

"If you're sure, but your father and I love you, and we'd love to help. . ." Megan cringed at the wistful tone in her mother's voice.

"I know. I love y'all too." The words sounded clipped, but they were all Megan could manage without breaking down.

"Well, then, we'll be praying for you and our sweet grandbaby too."

Megan bit back a sob. "That would be wonderful."

"Bye then."

"Bye." She mashed the button and allowed the sobs to come.

Her mother had invested her inheritance in her son-in-law's dreams and lost it, yet her concern was for her daughter. But Megan couldn't face her. Not until she could pay her back.

The doorbell rang, and for a fleeting moment, Megan had the crazy thought that her mother had shown up in person. Like she could drive ninety miles in two minutes.

Megan swiped at her tears and eased out of the rocker with the sleeping baby still on her shoulder. She pulled the front door open. Two men in suits stood on the porch. Their grim faces had her grabbing the doorframe for support.

"Mrs. Watson?"

"Yes?" Her heart thudded against her ribs.

Their expressions remained stony as they each flashed a badge. "We need to ask you some questions about your involvement in your husband's business."

one

Senator Holt McFadden knew the dangers of praying for patience, but the silent plea he aimed heavenward was the petition of a desperate man. No one tested his forbearance like Marshall Whitmore. Holt had attempted to break all ties with the man who'd almost become his father-in-law, but Marshall refused to stop pestering him to vote according to his own private agenda.

The current cell phone conversation was no exception. Though he needed to make a deposit, Holt had parked two blocks from the bank so he could soak in the beauty of the perfect spring day in the heart of his district as he walked. Instead, he'd been subjected to Marshall's badgering the entire time.

"You have to think about others, Holt. You can't just go off on some Pollyanna crusade for old folks. What about those of us who are trying to eke out a living the best way we can?"

"You know, Marshall, you're not even in my district. Have you told Mike Bradley how you feel about things? He would really be the one you need to talk to."

"Don't play games with me, Holt. Bradley doesn't have the influence you do, and you know it. I'm not asking you to compromise those *values* you hold so dear. I'm just offering a way we can all win."

In spite of his exasperation, Holt grinned. Only Marshall could make values sound like an ugly word.

He cradled the cell phone against his shoulder, trying to tune out Marshall's insistent drone. He wished he could just hang up, but unfortunately, the man did have a lot of political pull. Reverting to a habit left over from his childhood, he studied the cracks in the sidewalk as his feet cleared them, taking care not to step on a single one.

"Oomph." He grunted against the impact and looked up, helpless to stop the phone as it flew from his hand. A myriad of brightly hued fabrics cascaded to the sidewalk in front of him. Sprawled in the middle of the splash of color, a young woman gazed up at him with eyes that exactly matched the blue of the May sky.

He dropped to his knees beside her. "Are you okay?"

She nodded slowly and eased herself into a sitting position, pushing long blonde hair off her face with a slender hand. "I think so. Nothing seems to be broken." Her shy smile hinted at dimples. "I'm sorry I didn't —"

"I'm sorry I wasn't —"

They each nodded for the other to go ahead.

"—see you," she said. Her smile grew wider, confirming his dimple theory.

"—looking where I was going," Holt finished with a wry grin. He retrieved the phone lying beside her on the concrete, amazingly unharmed. Shaking his head in disbelief, he pushed END to be sure Marshall was really gone. "I was on the phone."

She hurried to gather her scattered belongings, then grimaced as her gaze fell on some broken porcelain pieces. Disappointment flashed across her face.

Holt suddenly realized that, in spite of her petite frame, she was older than he'd first thought. Closer to his own age.

She shrugged, her easy smile returning, and retrieved a gold hair-clip from the sidewalk. "Great. The one time I decide to carry my bolts of fabric instead of going around to the loading dock, I run into one of those cell phone maniacs you hear about."

Holt watched in awe as her nimble fingers twisted her hair into an upswept style and secured the long tresses.

Her hand froze in place as if she was struck motionless by a thought. "Wait a minute." Her eyes twinkled with mischief. "Aren't you people just supposed to be dangerous drivers? I've never heard of any warnings about pedestrian cell phone use. There ought to be a law."

He chuckled and helped her to her feet. "As soon as the senate is back in session, I'll speak to my colleagues about passing a law against it on your behalf."

She abruptly dropped his hand. "You're a senator." It wasn't even a question. More like a statement of disgust.

Resisting the urge to flinch, Holt reminded himself that even his own family had struggled with his chosen career. Prejudice against politicians was something he ran into frequently. Usually the direct approach worked best. "I admit it. I'm a state senator, but other than that, I'm a pretty nice guy. Here, I'll even prove it." He hefted her fabric up before she could protest. "Where were you headed with these?"

"Over there." She nodded toward an older model red minivan, but the lack of emotion on her face made him feel like a bag boy at the supermarket.

He loaded the material into the back seat. Unwilling to lose the easy camaraderie they'd established when they first bumped into each other, he forged on. "How about a cup of coffee? It's the least I can do for knocking you down. There's a little place right around the corner. . ."

When she avoided eye contact with him, Holt knew she was slipping away. She shook her head. "Thanks, but I'd better not. I left my daughter with a neighbor."

He instinctively glanced at her left hand, then felt heat rush to his face as her gaze followed his.

"I'm a widow." Now her blue eyes confronted his without wavering under the scrutiny.

"I'm sorry, Mrs. . . ." He let his voice drift off and held his breath waiting for her to fill in the implied blank, then blew it out in soft disappointment when she didn't.

"It's been three years. I've become accustomed to it, but thank you for your sympathy and your help." Her gentle smile eased the awkwardness, but the formal words signaled an end to the conversation as she slid under the steering wheel, closed the door, and started the motor.

"Wait!" He thanked God for a town where people left their windows rolled down in the summer.

"Yes?" She paused in mid-act of slipping on the black sunglasses she'd removed from the rearview mirror.

"I'm Holt. . .Holt McFadden."

"Yes, I recognized you after you said you were a senator. Nice meeting you."

She let the sunglasses drop into place on her pert little nose. His own slightly frustrated expression reflected back at him from the mirrored lenses.

"And you are. . . ?"

"Late to pick up my daughter." With a wave, she eased onto the road and sped down the highway, fading into a tiny dot of red.

Holt stood, rooted to the spot, watching the van disappear on the horizon. Why hadn't she told him her name?

≈

Megan Watson hurried up her neighbor's wooden steps and banged on the rickety screen door.

"Come on in. It's open."

"Open? Of course. Why would I expect anything else?" Megan muttered to herself, frowning as she entered the house. "Aunt Irene, how many times have I told you. . . ? I could have been an ax murderer." Megan worked hard to maintain her scowl. Not an easy task, when she was confronted with that precious wrinkled face, wreathed in smiles.

"Too many times, Honey. Tell me again, and I might just have to call the police." The wizened old woman winked and turned back to the pie crust dough on the Formica counter. After a few seconds of energetic rolling pin use, she paused in midstroke and swung around. Her gaze searched Megan's face. "Now, Meg, don't you go pale on me, Girl. I didn't mean nothin' by that, and you know it."

Megan rewarded her elderly friend with a rueful grin. "I'm not about to 'go pale' on you. I'm tougher than I used to be." As she spoke, she realized it was true. Even a joke about calling the authorities would have made her 'go pale' a year ago, but she'd come a long way since then. "You'd have to actually call the police before I'd get scared." She looked around the spotless kitchen. "Where's my little rapscallion? You get tired of her and sell her to the egg man?"

"Very funny, young lady. You wouldn't talk so smarty to me if your grandma was still alive." The gray-haired woman wiped her flour-covered hands on the faded cotton towel that hung from the cabinet door handle.

"No, sirree, you got that right. She wouldn't have allowed me to sass you. Only she could do that."

"That's right, and don't you forget it." Aunt Irene wrapped Megan in a hug, smoothing the younger woman's hair with a papery hand. "Your little one is sound asleep in the den. She's all tuckered out from chasin' the pups, I reckon."

The two women walked arm in arm into the den and

stood silently admiring the tiny girl, dozing contentedly among four snoring Golden Retriever puppies.

"Looks like she wore them out too," Megan whispered. "Sorry I didn't make it back from town before her naptime." *I would have, if not for my little run-in with the senator.*

She'd spent the whole trip home banishing him from her mind. The last thing she needed was to get involved with a public figure. Or anyone else, for that matter. She grunted in disgust as the charming man wormed his way back into her thoughts. She hadn't had even a passing interest in anyone since Barry's death, and now she was reeling like an awestruck teenager after a five-minute encounter with this man.

Ignoring the older woman's puzzled look, she turned the grunt into a small cough. "I'll try to get her out to the van without disturbing her. I've got to get Mrs. Wallace's quilt done before tomorrow."

"Ah, Child, now you do sound like your Granny Lola. Always hurryin' to finish quiltin' somebody's precious quilt top." Megan pretended not to notice the tears that sprang to Aunt Irene's eyes whenever she spoke of her best friend and neighbor of fifty years. The elderly woman didn't want to be pitied. "The good Lord knows I'm grateful to have you for a neighbor, Honey. But I don't know if Lola gave you a blessing or a curse when she left you her little house and that big old quilting machine."

"Yes, you do know. If it weren't for those two things, I don't know what we'd have done after. . .after Barry's death," Megan whispered, mindful of her sleeping daughter.

"Yes, but you're young. When are you going to quit hiding, Child? You didn't do anything wrong. You need to get out more. . .not be chained to a quilting machine twenty-four hours a day." Aunt Irene's melodramatic word picture elicited a muffled giggle from both women that broke the melancholy mood. "But since you insist on being a slave to the business, why don't you let Sarah stay here while you do your work?"

Tempted to agree, Megan took a good look at her eighty-year-old neighbor. Fatigue showed in her weather-beaten face, in spite of her cheerful words. Keeping up with Sarah was hard work. "I'd better take her today. Maybe next time. Thanks, though."

❧

"Home at last," Megan muttered, putting the gearshift in park and killing the motor. She cast a glance to the back where Sarah still snoozed in her car seat. Slight for her four years, what the preschooler lacked in size, she made up for in energy.

As Megan eased her daughter out of the restraint, she thanked God for her tiny blessing, then carried her into the bedroom they shared and tucked her into the toddler bed. Turning to tiptoe out of the room, she froze as a thin, high-pitched voice rang through the silence.

"I was just resting my eyes."

Sarah's battle cry. She never wanted to admit she was actually sleeping. It was a point of honor with the little girl. This time, though, her fatigue was stronger than her will, and she nestled farther into the covers, breathing evenly again.

Megan turned on the monitor—Sarah wouldn't tolerate her calling it a baby monitor anymore—and clipped the receiver to her belt.

She walked outside and stopped for a minute to breathe in the fresh air and soak in the solitude. Unbidden, the memory of Holt McFadden intruded on her peaceful thoughts. Never seeing him again was her only option. She should be proud of herself for ensuring that by not telling him her name. So why had disappointment woven its way into her heart instead?

Pulling her mind back to the present, she grabbed the fabric from the van. She hurried with it into the sewing room where childhood memories were as tangible as the rows of thread spools and bolts of material that lined the floor-to-ceiling shelves. Watching her grandmother quilt on the big machine had always fascinated Megan. Hard to believe Granny Lola had been gone three-and-a-half years.

At first, she'd wondered what she would do with it, but amid the turmoil after Barry's death, Megan had been immeasurably grateful for the inheritance of the small farm-house and huge quilting machine. She'd poured her heart into her new business.

God saw to it she had enough. Enough for what she had to do and enough left over for her and Sarah to live on. A little frugality on her part and they got along just fine.

After she put away her supplies, she carefully loaded Mrs. Wallace's quilt top onto the machine. Stitching around each basket enhanced the beauty of the quilt, but it was much more tedious than doing a basic design on the whole surface. She'd be hard pressed to get it done by tomorrow as promised. She wouldn't hurry, though. The delicate hand-pieced quilt top deserved her best work.

Just as Megan's shoulders began to ache from guiding the needle along the fabric, Sarah ran into the room with a drowsy smile.

"Mama! Somebody's here."

Megan switched off the machine. "Did you look out the window?"

Sarah nodded, her blond hair bobbing up and down.

"Who is it?"

"I don't know. He's tall, though, Mama. Sort of like a prince." Excitement danced in Sarah's eyes.

Megan grinned. "But what would a prince be doing so far from his kingdom, O Fair Maiden?"

Their visitor was hardly a prince, she was sure, but considering the quiet area they lived in, most likely not a villain, either. Probably either a book salesman or someone lost in the winding backroads of rural Arkansas, looking for directions to town.

The last thing she felt like doing was facing a stranger. For a second, she considered not answering the sharp rap that resounded through the cottage. Her conscience rebelled, though, when she realized the man had probably seen Sarah's little face looking out the window.

She ruffled her daughter's hair. "Come on, Squirt. Let's go see who it is."

Sarah giggled and danced along beside her as they hurried down the hallway to the front door.

A terrifying thought scurried through Megan's mind, halting her forward momentum. She got down on her knees and grasped Sarah gently by the shoulders. "What did the man look like, Honey?" she asked, lowering her voice to a whisper.

With a scowl, Sarah shrugged and tried to wiggle out of her mother's grip. "Tall, I told you," she said, imitating Megan's whisper. "But he looked nice, Mama."

"What color was his hair?" Megan held her breath as she waited for the four year old to answer.

"I'm not sure. . ." Sarah squirmed again and gazed intently at her mother.

"It wasn't red?"

"You mean like Derek's, at Sunday school?"

Megan nodded, and when Sarah shook her head decisively, Megan relaxed her hold and smoothed her daughter's blouse. Rising on legs that felt like cooked spaghetti, she fought back the anger. Ivo Pletka's vengeful articles had stopped two years ago, and she'd thought he had lost the ability to terrorize her, but at the least expected moment, his smug, hateful face materialized in her thoughts.

Dear Lord, please let me learn to trust again. Sarah doesn't deserve to have a mother who's always on edge. I've got to lighten up. "Are you ready to meet the mysterious prince?" she asked her daughter, with a chuckle.

She peeked out the window beside the door. The forced laugh died on her lips. Worse than a salesman. A politician. A handsome one who appeared to be bearing gifts.

two

Holt rarely had trouble finding the right words for any situation, but what did a man say when he showed up on a beautiful woman's doorstep, uninvited and obviously unwanted? Somehow, he didn't think that was covered in *The Senator's Book of Etiquette*. He cleared his throat and opened his mouth, willing something intelligent to come out. "Hey, Mrs. Watson."

She nodded, arms crossed, blue eyes steady, apparently content to let him squirm like a worm on a hook. Her scrutiny alone wouldn't have been so bad, but right beside her, arms in an identical position, stood a miniature version of Megan Watson, matching her mother scowl for scowl. Hoping to break through at the weakest link, Holt squatted down in front of the smaller edition. "And you must be Sarah."

The little girl simply nodded, and Holt began to wonder if anyone else was going to speak. He produced the larger of his two packages and held it out to her. "I have something here to make up for bumping into your mama in town earlier. I didn't want you to be left out, so I brought you something too."

Her eyes widened. She reached toward the package but quickly retracted her hand and tucked it behind her back. Her mute glance sought her mother's permission, and Holt watched Megan's steely gaze soften.

"It's okay, Sarah." At her mother's words, Sarah reached out again and quickly grabbed the gift bag. "Tell Senator McFadden thank you, though."

"Thank you." Sarah tore into the bag with abandon, and the two adults watched the delight play across her face. "Coloring pencils! And a new drawing pad!"

Megan's head jerked up to meet Holt's gaze. "How'd you know what to get her?" With an incredulous little laugh, she continued, "I assumed you went to the DMV and used your influence to find me, but surely they couldn't tell you my little girl loves to draw."

"To tell you the truth, I did think of going to the Department of Motor Vehicles. I memorized your license number when you left today." Holt grinned, remembering how excited he'd been to realize he could locate the mystery woman that way. "But then I decided it wouldn't look good if I appeared to be throwing my influence around. Besides, since I was going into the quilting store anyway. . ." He tossed her the tiny wrapped package. "I decided I'd just ask Mrs. Sampson." At her raised eyebrows, he explained. "She's my cousin's mother-in-law."

"I stand amazed." She shook her head. "It really is a small world, isn't it?"

"Yes, Ma'am, we're all tied together tighter than rabbits in a tow sack."

"Is that the kind of jargon that won you the election, Senator?" A smirk played on her bow-shaped mouth, and Holt was taken off guard by the surge of emotion he felt.

"Please call me Holt. And I have to admit, that probably played a part in it." He grinned. "That and my muddy four-wheeler and pickup truck full of coon dogs." Clearing his throat, he tossed in some truth. "Of course, my desire for the folks around here to have a say in the laws might have helped some."

He watched in anticipation as she looked down at Sarah,

who sat coloring on the step, then brought her crystal gaze back to meet his. "Want to come in for a glass of tea?"

ᴥ

Megan carefully placed two tall glasses of ice and a half-full tea pitcher on the round golden oak table in the corner of the living room. She smiled at her guest, even as her heart pounded. "Thanks, again, for getting Sarah coloring pencils. She really does love to draw."

"So do I." Holt's eyes crinkled with amusement.

Amazing how the tiny crow's feet at the corners somehow make him look more joyful, Megan thought as she sank down in a chair next to him.

"Always have," he continued. "I remember when I was little. . .my mama would threaten to get me if I didn't quit coloring on the wall. I'd hear my daddy calming her down. 'Leave him alone,' he'd say, 'you think Picasso's mom yelled at him?' 'Picasso probably didn't have two little brothers following in his footsteps,' she always answered. She'd fuss a little more, but eventually, she gave me one section of wall for my very own. If I drew on the wall outside of that spot, I knew I was in trouble."

Megan laughed and poured the two glasses full of tea. "Don't you dare tell Sarah that story." She playfully shook her finger at him. "She'd better not start drawing on the walls, or I'll know who to blame."

"Hmm. . .corrupting small children. . .nope, don't guess even this old politician would stoop that low."

Ignoring his jibe, she asked, "So, did you pursue art when you were older?"

"Nah, not professionally. I took some art classes in college, but business management seemed a little steadier. Then I sort of fell into politics." He waggled his eyebrows. "Not to be confused with falling into a pile of ticks, which is a good bit itchier."

She bit back a giggle and nodded, careful to keep a straight face. "But probably not any more dangerous." Allowing the smile she'd been restraining to blossom, she asked, "How does one 'fall into politics'?"

"I can tell you how it happened for me. I came home from college, sent off my résumé, and worked with Mom and Dad on the farm for awhile. One day, an old teacher of mine from high school came by, all upset. He told me the state senator for our district was in poor health and about to retire."

Holt sipped his tea. "An election was coming up and rumor had it the only replacement on the horizon was a liberal young man with radical ideas on everything from ecology to education. Thing was. . .they were afraid he might win just because it seemed that the voters wanted somebody young." He shook his head with a rueful grin. "I prayed a lot about it, and the rest, as they say, is history."

In spite of his joking, she sensed he had a deep commitment to his service in public office. Little did he know he was making conversation with a woman who could ruin his career by association. Maybe he wouldn't ever have to find out.

Suddenly she became aware of the silence.

He was staring at her. How long had she been quiet? She pushed the rewind button in her brain and replayed his last words, thanking God for this ability, which her family had always marveled at. Forcing a smile, she spoke, "Obviously it was a good fit. You've been in office how long? Almost three years?"

He nodded and finished his tea.

Setting her own empty glass down on the tiny table, Megan rose. She crossed the room and peeked out the screen door where Sarah sat on the porch, still absorbed in her art.

When she turned back to the living room, she shook her head. The man had been inside her house for fifteen minutes, making small talk, and she couldn't believe how much she'd relaxed. No wonder he'd won that last election by a landslide.

"Aren't you going to open it? I promise it won't bite."

Megan looked at him, puzzled. Then her gaze fell on the package that lay forgotten on the table. "Very funny. With your track record, it'll probably knock the breath out of me." She studied him as she eased the paper from the delicately wrapped tiny box. Most of her surprises in the last few years had been unpleasant.

After opening the box, she forced herself to breathe. A porcelain thimble peeped out at her—an exact replica of the shattered one she'd retrieved from the sidewalk after their collision. "Oh, Holt, thank you." She cringed, her cheeks growing hot at her reflexive use of his first name.

"Annie Sampson knew immediately what I was talking about when I described the broken one. She said you collect them."

"Annie Sampson said a lot, didn't she?" She hoped her joking tone didn't betray her fear. His face revealed no knowledge of her terrible secrets, so she barreled on. "Thank you for your thoughtfulness, Senator."

He ran his hand through his hair and offered a self-effacing smile. "Please stop calling me Senator. I assure you I'm not here in an official capacity."

Megan walked over and carefully added the newest addition to her thimble collection shelf. She turned back to face the man who sat so naturally at her table and tried for a casual tone. "In what capacity are you here?"

Their gazes held, and the silence again stretched to the point of being uncomfortable. Finally, Holt spoke. "You seemed like someone I'd like to get to know better. A neighborly visit appeared to be in order."

Her heart skittered over the implications of the first half of his solemnly spoken explanation and latched on to the last. "Neighborly?" She raised her eyebrows. "I didn't know you lived around here."

He nodded. "About two-and-a-half miles down the road. I was raised over ten miles from here, but we bought the old Lancaster place out on Salado Creek five years ago." His smooth smile resurfaced.

Megan's stomach lurched. His obvious interest in her, along with the notable absence of a wedding band had led her to believe he was single. Plus, she hadn't remembered reading about a wife in the newspapers. *He's a politician, you goose,* she derided herself. *What did you expect?*

"How does your wife like it here?"

"My wife?" A puzzled frown wrinkled Holt's forehead, then cleared as he chuckled. "Oh, because I said 'We'? My parents and I bought the land for our cattle, they have the ranch house already and a summer cottage in Lake Haven, so a little while back, I ended up moving in the house. We're still partners in the business, though. That's what I meant. Sorry."

Megan's frantic gaze lit on the empty tea pitcher. Scooping it up, she stammered, "That's okay. I just misunderstood. If you'll excuse me, I'll make some more tea." She pushed the swinging door with her body, and once it closed behind her, she collapsed against the counter, holding the cold pitcher against her hot face. Why had she made him explain? Now it looked as if she cared whether he was married or not. Nothing like giving him the wrong idea. Or was it the wrong idea?

She slammed the pitcher down on the counter with more force than necessary. A quick perusal through the cabinets revealed an empty tea bag box. Resting her forehead against the oak cabinet door, she tried to figure out why she was so rattled. Just because she'd spent three years avoiding relationships and now there was a man in her living room whom she would very much like to get to know. . .was that any reason to be rattled?

"Is something wrong?"

Megan jerked her forehead away from the cabinet door and spun around to confront the man who was no longer in her living room. "Uh. . .no. I'm out of tea bags." *Well, Meg, you're certainly making this a moot point. No way will he be interested in a crazy lady.*

"Ah," he said, nodding as if that were a perfectly logical excuse for mental collapse. "I see." He smiled, and the world righted itself. "Is there anything I can do to help?"

"Not unless you have a hidden stash of tea bags in your truck." Megan rolled her eyes at her own silliness. "Seriously, if you're still thirsty, I can make some lemonade."

"I'm not, but thanks." Pointing out the window at the glowing sun beginning its descent behind the mountains, he asked, "You and Sarah want to take a walk? I love this time of day."

Megan wanted to say yes. But this man had shared his heart with her about a career that obviously meant the world to him. How could she encourage him to jeopardize it by associating with her? Especially when he didn't even realize that was a danger. "Holt, I'd love to, and there's nothing Sarah likes better, but we just can't. I have work to do."

"I understand. Must be time to feed the chickens or something and here I am monopolizing you." He pushed open the kitchen door and held it as she slipped past him into the living room.

"Thank you for the gifts."

"It's the least I could do for mowing you down. Thank you for the tea. I really enjoyed our talk."

"Yes, me too." She fought to keep the wistfulness from her voice as she opened the screen door for him to go out.

They both glanced at the bottom mesh that curled out at one corner. Megan smiled and stepped out on the porch behind him. "When Sarah was barely able to walk, I'd lock this so she could see outside but still be safe. She spent hours pushing against the screen with her hands. Gradually it gave way."

He glanced over to where Sarah was still coloring, then back at Megan. "I admire persistence. Most of the time it pays off."

"But if that had been a wooden door, it would have been a waste of time," Megan said, recognizing his inference. She stepped off the porch into the yard, so he would do likewise.

Apparently taking the hint, he moved on towards his truck. "Bye, Megan. It was nice meeting you. Even nicer the second time."

"You too."

She sank down beside Sarah and tried to concentrate on the picture her daughter was drawing, instead of thinking about the man who was driving away—out of her life—just as she'd wanted.

three

"Marshall, I understand your position. But you have to understand mine. I can't vote against my constituents." Holt shifted in his chair to face the man squarely.

Marshall rose and slapped his hands palm down on the mahogany finish of the desk. "Now, see here—"

"I do see here, Sir," Holt said, careful not to raise his voice to one of the most influential men in Little Rock. He stood. "I'd like to help you, and I wish you the best of luck with your business, but I'm afraid that's the most I can do."

Instead of retreating, Marshall leaned in even closer to Holt's face, his hot breath punctuating each menacing word. "You think you'd be in the position you're in now if it weren't for me, Holt? Sure, you were a little Podunk senator, but you would never have chaired committees like you have if it weren't for my influence behind you." His mouth twisted in a bitter snarl. "To borrow a phrase from those hillbillies you're so fond of, it's not very smart to bite the hand that feeds you. I've been patient with you, in spite of your callous treatment of my daughter, but if you won't help me, I can get you out and get someone in who can."

Thinking of the countless hours spent campaigning, and the months of his life sacrificed serving and chairing various committees in order to make Arkansas a better place to live, Holt felt his own ire rise to the surface. How could this man, who admittedly had mentored him, take total credit for his success?

Especially considering he now knew for a fact how selfish Marshall's—and his daughter's—interest in him had been.

Determined to control the anger building inside him at the remembered betrayal, Holt remained calmly seated in his chair and dropped his gaze to the papers in front of him. His eyes didn't see the print, though, as he prayed for God to keep him calm. When he finished his petition for patience, he slowly rose and walked to the door. "I'm sorry you see it that way, Marshall," he said softly and opened the door.

The distinguished businessman straightened and turned, anger radiating from his body. "You'll be sorry, all right," he muttered and swept past Holt into the hallway.

Holt shook his head. What he needed right now was a big dose of sunshine. And he knew just where to find it.

ঌ

Megan pulled a clothespin out of her apron and fastened the corner of a towel to the sagging line. She was going to have to replace the middle post. It had rotted beyond redemption.

She preferred the softness of the dryer, but on sunny days like today, she'd hang a load on the line until they were almost dry then finish them in the dryer with a softener sheet. It was much more economical.

Besides when she put on Granny Lola's apron with the big pockets for clothespins, it was almost like slipping back into an easier, more carefree time. Life became simple again. Hanging out clothes brought back happy memories that were even more precious than the dollars she saved on the electric bill.

"When we get our puppy from Aunt Irene, I'm going to name him Rascal. Don't you think that's a good name, Mama?" Sarah pulled on Megan's apron.

Megan smiled. Sarah had been asking for a puppy ever since they were born. Even though she hadn't gotten an affirmative answer, lately she always spoke of "when we get our puppy." Holt McFadden's admiration of Sarah's persistence came to mind.

Why did everything these days remind her of that man? Even her prayers were filled with requests for God to help her forget him. If only his obvious integrity hadn't spoken to something deep inside her heart. It would have been easy to stop thinking about a smooth politician. A man devoted to serving his country was proving harder to put out of her mind.

"Mama, somebody's coming down the driveway."

Megan spun around. It had taken him a week, but Holt McFadden had decided to prove his persistence.

He got out of his truck, and the first thing she noticed was his cowboy hat. The second thing was his toolbox.

"Hello," he called across the yard.

"Hello."

"Thought I'd drop by and fix that screen for you, if that's okay."

Megan nodded dumbly.

He stopped when he drew closer and just looked at her. When he grinned, she drew herself up to her full 5'1" and glared at him. "What are you grinning at?"

"You."

"What's funny about the way I look?" Even as she asked, she remembered the too big apron.

"Nothing funny. You just look. . . ," he actually looked uncomfortable for the first time since she'd met him, then he recovered his grin, ". . .like a kid playing dress up."

"Did you drive over here just to make fun of me?" She didn't know why his appraisal had left her so breathless.

"No, I told you. I came to fix the door." He glanced at

Sarah who had stopped playing to watch the odd exchange between her mama and the man who'd obviously already won her four-year-old heart with coloring pencils and a drawing pad. "I sure could use a helper."

"I'll help." Sarah fairly bounced over to where Holt stood on the porch. "Can I?"

"Sure can." He looked at Megan. "If it's okay with your mama."

Megan put her hand up to shade her eyes and met his questioning gaze. They stood for a moment just looking at each other. His earlier comments about persistence pounded in her head. Finally, she nodded and looked down at the basket still half-full of towels. She had work to do herself. Trying to ignore the earnest conversation coming from the porch, as well as her own swirling emotions, she continued to pin towels on the line. Life had just become complicated again.

❧

Holt hammered on the frame that was stubbornly refusing to stay in place. The noise was loud, but at least it covered the sound of his heart banging in his chest. When he first saw Megan standing by the clothesline in her white apron, the light breeze playing in her long blond hair, he'd thought his heart was going to stop. Instead, it had started this incessant hammering.

The clothesline spoke of a simpler time, and standing next to it, Megan looked like the picture of wholesomeness—all that was fresh and innocent and wonderful personified. Even though he understood the danger she might inadvertently be to his career, she'd literally taken his breath away. He just prayed he'd have the strength to stand against any criticism that might come her way.

"Are we done?"

Holt looked up. Sarah pointed to the frame. He couldn't believe it. He'd been daydreaming. "No. I just needed to think." That was true.

He pulled out the cordless drill and tried the stubborn screw one more time. He smiled with relief when it eased in. Sarah held the frame, and he quickly spun the other screws into place. They soon had it mounted back in the screen door.

"I can't believe how long I let that go like that."

He spun around. Megan stood with an empty laundry basket on her hip.

"Not very many people hang out clothes anymore."

"No, I guess not. Did you know the dryer takes more electricity than most of your other appliances?"

"Yeah, I'd heard that." He was struck by how frugal she was compared to most women her age. He knew she'd been through some tough times, but he'd thought she came out okay financially. Was money that tight? Or did she just try to be frugal?

An uncomfortable silence stretched across the porch.

Sarah tugged on his belt loop. "I'm going to name my puppy Rascal."

He looked down at her with a smile. "Oh, really? When are you getting a puppy?"

Megan grinned and tousled Sarah's hair. "Nobody knows, but Sarah has apparently decided if she talks about it as a fact, it will happen." Sarah said something about telling her friend, Lucy, about Rascal and ran on inside. Megan glanced up at him. "Persistence, you know."

"Hey, sometimes it works."

"And sometimes it doesn't." She opened the repaired screen door and looked at it admiringly. "I appreciate you fixing that. How much do I owe you?"

"A cold drink of water?"

"Sure." She bit her lip, and he could almost see her mind working. "The water hose is right over there. It comes straight out of the well, so it's as cold as it gets."

She turned to go in, then pivoted back around to meet his gaze. "That screen was there for a reason. There were things outside that were dangerous to Sarah. Persistence isn't always a good thing."

Before he could reply, she went into the house, leaving him staring at the closed screen door he'd just repaired.

He could wait until he got home to get a drink.

ða

Holt hated staying inside on a beautiful day. Still, he'd promised himself he would make five calls today to drum up support for the bill he was planning on introducing to provide more benefits for the elderly. He'd hit a lot more opposition than he'd expected, but he was still determined to meet his goal. Thankfully, he'd saved his good friend, Chad Reynolds, for last. He was pretty sure Chad would give his support. He shared Holt's concern for senior citizens.

"Hello?"

"Chad, how are you? This is Holt."

"I can't complain. How about you?"

"I'm doing fine, Chad. You probably know why I'm calling. I was hoping I could count on your support for my bill."

"Well. . .I'm not really sure." The uncomfortable note in his friend's voice raised Holt's hackles. He'd noticed the same thing in the others voices but hadn't known them well enough to be positive.

"Be straight with me, Chad. Someone lobbying against me?"

"Uh. . .you might say that."

"Did Marshall Whitmore call you?"

"Yeah, he did." Relief filled Chad's voice. "I wanted to call and tell you, but I hated to."

"What did he say?"

"He's had an accountant do some figuring on your plan. He says your numbers are off, and we just can't afford it."

"There's nothing wrong with my numbers." Holt fought to keep the anger out of his voice. If he acted irrational now, that would play right into Marshall's hands. "I'll be glad to come by and go over them with you sometime soon."

"That sounds good. I couldn't believe he was right about you not researching it well enough, but he was convincing, I'll tell you that."

"I understand. I appreciate your being honest with me, Chad."

"No problem."

Holt hung up the phone. If Marshall thought he was that easily intimidated, he had better think again. He was thankful that was the last phone call. All he wanted was to get outside, and in spite of their less-than-perfect good-bye yesterday, he had at least one more thing to take care of at Megan Watson's.

❧

The following afternoon, Megan stared out the kitchen window. Holt McFadden was replacing the center support to her clothesline. As she watched, he vigorously drove a large punch bar into the ground around the rotten post. Even from here, she could see his shirt was wet.

Thankfully, Sarah was taking her nap, so Megan didn't have to worry about her begging to go out and see Holt. Her daughter talked about the man regularly in her conversations with her imaginary friends. There was no way she'd allow Megan a moment's peace if she knew he was outside.

Unfortunately, Megan wasn't allowing herself a moment's peace anyway. All she could think of was how awful she'd felt when he left the last time without even a cold glass of water. What kind of person was she? She'd been trying to protect him from her past, but surely, she could have given him a drink first.

She yanked open the refrigerator door and grabbed some lemons from the crisper. As soon as she'd squeezed them into a pitcher, she added sugar and water. She stirred the mixture briskly, then poured in some ice cubes for good measure. She couldn't get involved, but she could at least be polite. Holt McFadden wouldn't leave here thirsty this time.

She peeked out the window again. The center post had broken off about halfway down, the rotten part lying in pieces at Holt's feet. He leaned hard against the remaining stub. She watched him reposition himself around it, pushing, until at last it folded onto the ground.

Now looked like a good time for a break. She clipped the monitor onto her belt and grabbed two glasses from the cabinet. With them in one hand and the pitcher of lemonade in the other, she made her way out to the clothesline.

"Hello."

He turned around. "Hey." His gaze took in the lemonade and glasses. "Something wrong with the well?"

She flinched at his sarcasm, but she knew she deserved far worse. "Thank you for doing this. I thought you might want some lemonade."

"Sure." His brief flare of irritation seemed to have disappeared.

She poured him a drink, and by unspoken agreement, they moved up to the shade of the porch and sat in the side-by-side rockers.

"Why'd you do this after the way I treated you last time?"

He took a big gulp of his lemonade. "I wanted to see you again."

"It would be best if you didn't."

"Is that what you want?"

Her pulse quivered as his deep blue eyes regarded her closely. "It would be best."

She stood, her full glass of lemonade in one hand and the pitcher in the other.

"Wait." He motioned for her to stop.

"What?"

"When are you going to stop running?"

It was an honest question from an honest man. He deserved an honest answer. "Probably never." She turned back toward the door. The best thing she could do for him would be to quit worrying about whether he was thirsty or not.

"Megan."

She paused with her fingers on the door handle. "Yeah?"

"A person can't have too many friends."

She spun around to meet his gaze. "You want to be friends?"

He nodded, and it was impossible to doubt the sincerity in his eyes.

Her legs were trembling, but surely, he couldn't be hurt by a simple friendship with her. What would it be like to have a friend close to her age to visit with? She'd been lonely for so long, and after years of living under the cloud of Barry's deceit, Holt's honesty was like a refreshing rain shower.

She looked at him again. Still damp from the physical labor on her behalf, he'd proven himself a friend whether she accepted his offer of friendship or not. *You have to say no.* "Okay."

He didn't speak for a minute, apparently surprised by her

consent. Little did he know he wasn't nearly as shocked as she was.

Finally, he found his voice. "So how about we go for a walk after awhile—you, me, and Sarah—and watch the sunset?"

She started to agree, but suddenly, she remembered the work she was supposed to have finished during Sarah's nap. "Actually, I have some quilting that has to be done by tomorrow."

"I see." Disappointment flashed in his eyes, and she knew he thought she was still playing games.

"Then I'll be free." She cringed as her words hung in the air, a desperate plea for a rain check if she'd ever heard one.

"If I come by about this time Thursday, would you and Sarah show me the farm?"

"We'd love to." Not a smart answer, but certainly the one her heart favored.

He pushed to his feet, and apparently sensing that she wasn't ready for him to come into the house again, he set his empty glass on the rocker arm. "I'd better get back to work. Thanks for the lemonade."

"Thank you for fixing my clothesline."

He tipped his hat to her, then shoved it back on his head and headed back to his job.

Megan remained on the porch for a few minutes, watching Holt work. She felt like she could stand there forever.

Friends, just friends, she reminded herself. A cricket chirped in the distance, and the bellowing of a tree frog offered a forecast of much needed rain. "Come on, rain. Come tonight, but just let the sun shine Thursday," she muttered, as she slipped into the house and let the screen door slam behind her.

four

Thursday afternoon Holt hurried into the hardware store for the third time in the past week-and-a-half. He nodded at a ruddy-faced man who was stacking cans of paint on an aisle display. "Good morning, Josiah."

"Senator. It's so good to see you again." In spite of the fact that Holt had just been in the store two days ago, Josiah Barclay hurried over to shake his hand. "I heard something a mite interestin' yesterday."

"You did?"

"Yes, Sir. I heard you might be running for governor after your term for senator is up." The store owner's beady eyes scrutinized Holt's face. "Any truth to that?"

"Well, Josiah, I don't have any plans in place for that right now. I'll let you know, though, if I throw my hat in the ring."

Of course, that wasn't promising much since he'd let the whole state know if he threw his hat in the ring. Then again, probably the best way to let the whole state know would be to tell Josiah. He and his wife, Barbara, could spread news faster than a forest fire—and were just as dangerous at times.

"You be sure you do." The man looked over his shoulder, and Holt had the distinct feeling Josiah's wife would likely torture him if he missed a juicy piece of gossip like their local senator running for governor.

"Senator McFadden, how good to see you." Holt turned around to find Barbara Barclay smiling at him.

"Hello, Barbara." Normally, he'd call her Mrs. Barclay, but

38

the age-conscious woman had told him long ago to use her first name.

"LaWanda is home from college for the summer. . ." She peered through her long black eyelashes at him. "Maybe you can come over for supper some night."

The Barclay's daughter, LaWanda, looked like a younger version of her mother. Many men considered that a good thing. But no one had been able to tolerate her sharp tongue for very long. Holt didn't intend to try, but since the Barclays were voters, he didn't want to alienate them.

"I appreciate the offer. This is really a busy time for me." He smiled to take the sting out of his refusal.

"Busy? Are you seeing someone?" Barbara cut straight to the heart of the matter.

He instinctively started to say no, but Megan Watson's face popped into his mind. "Kind of."

"Ohh. . ." Barbara's heavily made-up face contorted as the disappointment of losing a possible date for her daughter warred with delight over a tidbit of gossip concerning Holt.

Holt left her struggling with her emotions and turned his attention to the ropes. When he had the length he wanted, he paid quickly and practically ran out of the store.

He loved small towns. But sometimes gossip seemed to run rampant there much more than it did in a big city like Little Rock. In the city, you were only gossiped about by people in your own circle. Here everybody was open game.

Of course, if God saw fit to make him governor, he'd be open game anyway—three-hundred-sixty-five days a year, seven days a week, twenty-four hours a day. He struggled with the idea of so much scrutiny.

Public opinion was very important to him, but if he hoped to succeed, he would have to live his life, as much as possible, above reproach, then trust the Lord to take care of the rest.

Megan Watson's face flashed in his mind. How did she figure into God's plans for Holt's life?

As he walked down the sidewalk, shopkeepers called to him from their doorways, and he returned their waves. Yes, in small towns, people could be counted on to pull together in a pinch, but the flip side of that was they always thought they should know each other's business. No wonder Megan found it easier to hide out on her little farm.

❧

Megan pressed a hand to her stomach, hoping to calm the butterflies that had been cavorting there since lunch. This morning she'd been too busy finishing Mrs. Gaskin's quilt to think about Holt McFadden's scheduled visit. But as soon as the woman picked up the quilt and waved good-bye, the fluttering had begun.

Megan pulled out her favorite capris. Tiny pink flowers adorned the white material. She topped the pants with a bright pink shirt and slipped on her walking sandals. She ran a brush through her long hair and, after a glance in the mirror, decided on just a touch of lipstick. Compared to the well-coifed beauties that one normally associated with politicians, she looked terribly bland.

Her disappointing self-evaluation jerked to a halt at the honk of a horn. A peek out the window revealed Holt and Sarah exchanging merry waves. Megan shrugged once more at the mirror image. "You can't be more than friends anyway," she murmured. "Don't get bent out of shape." Shaking her head at the disparity between her wise advice and her churning emotions, she hurried down the hallway.

She opened the front door and stepped out on the porch. A

good rain shower from yesterday had brightened the trees and flowers and even the grass to radiant colors. But today, just as she'd wished, sunshine cascaded down in abundance. Her heart lightened, and she waved at the man in the cowboy hat.

"Got on your walking shoes?" she called, as she approached them.

Laughing, Holt lifted up his foot to reveal well-worn cowboy boots. "I can even run in these babies if the need arises."

"Hmm. . . Being a politician, I bet the need arises fairly frequently, huh?"

"I won't even honor that with a reply." He grinned. He glanced at Sarah playing near the porch with her doll. "Before we go, I need to ask you something."

Megan forced her face to remain calm. Had he heard something about her past? Was their friendship over before it had barely had time to begin? "Yes?"

He lowered his voice. "I had an old tire at home, and I bought some heavy rope at the hardware store." He pointed at a big tree in Megan's front yard. "I was thinking that old oak right there would be perfect for a tire swing." He grimaced. "If you don't mind."

Relief pushed the air out of her lungs, and it came out as an incredulous little laugh. "That would be great. Sarah would love it."

"Well, it's not a puppy, but it doesn't eat much and is pretty quiet." He tossed the words over his shoulder as he retrieved the tire and rope from the back of his truck. With them in his hands, he swung back around to face her. "I didn't want to mention it to Sarah without asking you first."

"I appreciate that. It's really nice of you to think of her." Megan fought back the suspicion that Holt felt sorry for Sarah due to their somewhat solitary life.

"What's that for?" Sarah had abandoned her doll and was staring at the rope and tire.

"We're going to put up a swing." He deftly knotted the rope and tossed it effortlessly over the high limb. In minutes, he had the tire swing fully operational.

Holt and Megan took turns pushing Sarah. She giggled hysterically with every pass but finally motioned for Holt to stop. He grabbed the tire and held it still while she got off.

"Now it's your turn, Mama."

Megan shook her head. "Oh, no, Honey. It won't hold me."

Holt nodded. "Actually, it will. Go ahead, Megan. Give it a try."

She cast him a doubtful glance, but he and Sarah were already propelling her forward to the tire. She climbed in, feeling incredibly awkward.

Holt grinned. "Hold on."

She nodded toward her hands clenched tightly around the rope. "Don't worry. I am."

He pulled the tire—with her on it—back as if it weighed no more than a pillow. Then he let go.

She gasped. The air whizzed by, and the bottom dropped out of her stomach. She was vaguely aware that he was continuing to push her, but for the most part, she was mindless. She closed her eyes and peace settled over her like a soft blanket.

Memories of swinging as a child came back, and she wondered how she could have ever forgotten this simple joy. Eventually, she became aware the swing was slowing down, pulling her back to the present. She opened her eyes. Holt and Sarah were beaming at her.

Regretfully, she allowed her feet to drag her to a complete stop. But when she eased out of the tire, her legs felt strangely noodle-like. "Whoa."

Holt grabbed her and slid his arm around her waist. She leaned in against him, relishing the pleasant smell of his aftershave. *This is only making the trembly feeling worse,* she thought, biting back a small giggle.

Mindful of her vow to be friends only, she stood up straight. "I'm okay now." When he released her, she offered a tremulous smile. "That was wonderful." Heat crept up her cheeks. Surely he would know she was referring to swinging.

"I'm glad you enjoyed it." Before she could decide if he was teasing her, Sarah threw her arms around her.

"Yeah, Mama, you looked like you were a princess."

Megan stared down at the precocious four year old. If she didn't change the subject, Sarah was sure to combine this analogy with the one that they'd made up before they knew who was at the door the first day Holt had visited. "So, who's ready for a walk?"

"I am! I am!"

Motioning at the expanse of rolling hills, Holt asked, "Where shall we start?"

"Let's go down to the creek, Mama, please!" Sarah flitted around Megan, bouncing up and down.

"Sounds like a plan, Hon." She chuckled as Sarah bounded down the path before she could finish her sentence. "I worry about her," she said, with a mock frown. "She's such a couch potato."

"I can see that." He fell into step beside her, and they enjoyed a companionable silence for awhile.

The four year old skipped ahead of Holt and Megan, stopping only to blow a "wishing flower" now and then, spreading dandelion seeds to the far corners of the property and beyond.

"So, have you always lived in this area?" Holt asked.

"This was my grandma's house. My mom's family is from

here." She measured her words, careful to reveal no more than she wanted to. When she was younger, she'd always loved to talk. But she'd spent the last three years speaking when she was spoken to and never volunteering information. Even a smooth-talking cowboy couldn't loosen her tongue. "I was raised in Jonesboro."

"Really?"

"Why do you sound so surprised?"

"I don't know." He kicked a loose pebble with his foot. "You just seem so at home here."

"That must be because I spent summers here. It was the highlight of my year." Surely this rugged country she loved would be a safe topic. She paused as they topped a small hill. "I was baptized there," she said, and nodded down at the creek below, "the summer I turned thirteen."

His eyes grew wide. "You're kidding." He shook his head. "I was baptized in this same creek, about ten miles down the road."

"Wow. It's that 'small world' thing again, isn't it?" In spite of her attempt to make light of the connection, Megan sensed a crack in the barrier she'd erected between them at the reve-lation that this man was a Christian. Mouth dry, she stood beside him, watching the water ripple over the smooth rocks.

"Have you ever thought of leaving here? Living somewhere else?" Megan asked. Then she turned to study the face of the man who seemed as much a part of the land as the rocks and trees.

"Thought about it once." Something that looked like pain flickered across his face. "Decided against it." He bent down, picked up a flat rock and, with a practiced move, skipped it across the water. His cowboy hat shaded his eyes, but Megan was sure she hadn't imagined the emotion.

"Must have been a pretty good offer for you to even con-sider it." Her burgeoning curiosity surprised her. The man was as mysterious as the nooks and crannies of the big rock bluff across the water, and probably as dangerous to explore.

"I guess I thought it was, until I realized how little I had to gain compared to how much I had to lose. So I stayed here." His eyes seemed to take measure of her soul, and she felt suddenly ruffled by his cryptic answers. Was he nursing a broken heart?

Sarah had given up dandelions in favor of collecting the tiny rocks along the beach, and her sudden cry broke the mood. "Come see this one, Mom. Look, Mr. Holt."

Megan and Holt obediently "oohed" and "aahed" over her latest find, then Megan sank down on a large jagged boulder.

Holt rested one foot on the slab, and they stared in silence at the rippling water.

Finally, he spoke. "Look at those rocks barely under the surface. They're so smooth they look like they've been hand polished."

"The water beats them down until they lose their identity in the current." Mesmerized by the constant flow, she had a sudden epiphany. "Sometimes the world feels like rushing water, doesn't it?"

Had she really said that aloud?

She looked up to find his dark blue eyes studying her intently, confirming that she had indeed spoken her thoughts. She quickly summoned a grin. "You'd better be careful. I hear it's especially that way in politics."

He looked as though he might delve deeper into her earlier comment but offered an answering smile instead. "I'm going to have to hang around just to change your mind about those of us in public service."

In spite of the impossibility of the statement, his words sent a tingle of anticipation down her spine.

five

Holt couldn't think of another excuse to show up at Megan's, but he couldn't stay away. When he drove up on Tuesday, he considered walking in with his toolbox and saying, "What needs fixing?"

Instead, empty-handed, he knocked lightly on the door. He saw Sarah peek out the front window, then heard the lock click. She pulled the door open and peered at him suspiciously. "Did Mama know you were coming?"

"I don't guess so. Is that okay?"

"I don't know. I don't think her hair is brushed. So she might be mad."

"Is she busy?"

"Nah, she's just quilting."

Holt bit back a grin at the four year old's priorities. He could hear the machine noise down the hallway. It stopped suddenly, and he heard footsteps on the hardwood floor.

"Sarah," Megan called. Just as she finished saying her daughter's name, she came around the doorway into the hall and skidded to a stop. "Holt. What are you doing here?" Her hand went to her hair. Sarah knew her mama well.

"I just dropped by to see if you needed anything, but since I'm here, may I ask a favor?"

"What?" Her tone was suspicious, and she still stood frozen in the hallway.

"Would you let me watch you quilt? I've never seen

46

anyone use one of those machines before, and I'd love to see it."

Hesitance clouded her face.

"Only for a few minutes," he asked. "So I can explain to my mama how you do it."

At the mention of his mother, she capitulated and motioned him brusquely to her sewing room. He noticed she smoothed her hair down with her hand one more time. He thought it looked beautiful, a little more unruly than she usually wore it. The extra fullness of her hair emphasized her delicate facial features.

"Sit there." Megan's abrupt words and motion toward a stool in the corner brought him back to the room. The quilting machine was even bigger than he imagined. It easily took up half the room. A desk on the other side had a sewing machine perched on top. Fabric was everywhere, giving the illusion of a kaleidoscope of colors. Compared to the sparseness of the rest of the house, this room seemed plush and luxurious.

He sat as directed and watched a master at work. Sarah came in, perched on his knee for awhile, then disappeared to her own room to play. Holt took this opportunity to stand and move in closer to the machine.

Standing, he could see the delicate stitches appearing on the fabric as if by magic when Megan moved the red laser light across the paper pattern on the shelf in front of the quilt. Her hands worked swiftly and surely. Holt could see she'd had lots of practice.

"Do you always use a pattern?"

She shook her hand and slipped one finger free. She held it up. "Just a minute."

He nodded and waited.

Soon she stopped. "That one's all done." He could see she was relaxing. "Want to see me do one freehand—without a pattern?"

"Sure." He was fascinated by the quilting process, but he knew in his heart he would have gladly watched her clean the rug if that's what it took to spend time with her. Then again, she didn't have a rug. Her feet were standing firmly on the hardwood floor. He wondered at the stamina it must take to put in as many hours at this as she obviously did a day.

She skillfully switched quilts and offered him a tentative smile. "Pay attention. There may be a test later."

He watched in amazement as she stitched around several different style birdhouses imprinted on the forest green material. She carefully followed the edges of the design then stopped and met his gaze. "Now it's your turn."

When she offered him the controls, he shook his head. "I might mess up your quilt."

"So? This is one I'm doing to sell, not a quilt top someone brought me. If you mess it up, you can just buy it from me." Her mischievous grin reminded him of Sarah.

"I don't have any quilts. Maybe that wouldn't be a bad idea. I'm not sure birdhouses are my thing though."

"No quilts?" She looked at him as if he'd said he had three noses. "Your grandmother never made you a quilt?"

He shook his head. "I guess she thinks a bachelor deserves to be cold." He grinned. "She does quilt, though. But she doesn't have a machine."

Megan's eyes brightened. "She hand quilts? My granny used to hand quilt. She'd spend ten times longer quilting one this size by hand." She patted the large quilt on the machine. "Of course, it was worth a lot more, but people around here couldn't afford to pay the bigger price. Granny hated going with a machine at first, but she finally agreed that comparing it with hand quilting was like comparing bacon and ham. Both of them are pork, and both are delicious, but they're just completely different."

"So do you hand quilt?"

"In my spare time?" She shook her head with a rueful grin. "No, but I really admire people who do." Her grin grew broader. "Come on and give this baby a try. Just think. You'll be able to tell your grandmother you quilted a quilt."

He glanced at the material. "Yes, a pink and yellow quilt, no less. I'm sure she'll be impressed."

"Trust me, she will."

Holt reached out tentatively toward the handles. Megan sighed, put her hands on his, and guided them to the correct place. At her touch, an almost electrical shock jumped through him, but he kept his eyes on the job at hand. She leaned up to reposition his fingers and the fruity scent of her shampoo assailed his senses. He was still careful not to react. She reminded him of a hurt kitten, and the last thing he wanted was to scare her off.

After a few false starts, he was able to do a painstakingly slow version of her work. He enjoyed it but was thankful when she took it back. She finished in silence, then turned the machine off and faced him. "Why are you really here?"

"I thought we might go for another walk."

"Wouldn't it have been easier to have just said that than to have suffered through home-ec class?"

"I enjoyed the quilting. It was kind of fun, really. Kind of reminded me of racquetball."

She shot him a look that let him know she thought he was crazy. "Uh-huh."

"Well, it's the eye/hand coordination thing. It works the same brain nerve-endings, I bet."

"Good thing you're a senator and not a doctor."

"If you're through doubting my medical knowledge, would you like to go for a walk?"

"I'd love to."

Megan called for Sarah to get ready to walk, then she looked at Holt. "Want to have a seat in the living room while I change into some walking clothes and shoes?"

"Sure." Holt strolled back to the living room. He couldn't help but notice how bare Megan's house was. Somehow, he'd expect a woman her age to have more. More furniture, more knick-knacks. . .he looked at the floor. . .more rugs, more everything.

As soon as he sat down, Sarah came in lugging a pair of tennis shoes. "Will you put these on me?" She climbed up in his lap.

"Can't you put them on yourself?"

"I can, but I don't want to. I'm gonna ask Mama for Velcro ones for my birthday, so I don't have to tie them."

"Really? When's your birthday?"

"July 23rd. But guess what?" The little girl's voice dropped to a whisper. "Mama's birthday is tomorrow!"

"Are you sure?"

The look she gave him was priceless. "I'm sure. Don'tcha think I know when Mama's birthday is?" She put her finger to her lips. "But don't tell."

He lowered his voice. "Why?"

"Cause I just remembered I'm not supposed to tell anybody."

He nodded and made a motion of locking his lips and throwing away the key. His dramatics had Sarah giggling so hard it was a struggle to put on her shoes. He got them on, though, and he and Sarah went outside to wait for Megan.

Five minutes later, Megan stepped out onto the porch. She had pulled her hair up in a long ponytail, but she knew the unruly curls were still evident. She saw Holt noticing. "I didn't blow dry it."

"What?"

"I didn't blow dry my hair. I usually try to straighten it, but I had a lot of quilting to do, so I just let it dry naturally today. It curls up really bad when I do that."

"Curls up 'really bad'? I think it's beautiful."

She felt her cheeks grow hot at his compliment. "Ready to walk?"

"Sure. Lead the way."

For the first five minutes or so, her embarrassment truly pushed her to "lead the way." Sarah scampered along beside her, and they left Holt several yards behind. But he soon caught up with them. "Whoa. I thought we were going for a walk. Didn't know that meant power walking."

"You have something against power walking? I thought you politicians were all for anything having to do with power."

He ignored her jibe and matched his stride to hers. "Is the creek your favorite spot on this land?"

"Close, but no, there's one other place I like better."

"Is it within walking distance?" He chuckled. "I'm almost afraid to ask. If we keep up this pace, there isn't much in the state that won't be within walking distance."

She bit back a grin and slowed down a little. "It's not far." After she yelled at Sarah, who, in spite of Holt's teasing complaint about the pace, was running ahead, they changed directions. As they approached her favorite spot, Sarah hung back and held onto her mother's hand.

"Amazing." Holt shook his head in awe at the view from the bluff. Down below, the creek twisted through the terrain like an earthworm trying desperately to return to its home underground.

The three hikers sat down together to watch the sun go down on the horizon. Pink and purple streaks crisscrossed the blue sky, and the fading orb cast an orange glow over the scene. Megan tried to concentrate on nothing but God's wondrous sunset, but she was painfully aware of the persistent man beside her. How would she ever convince him to leave her alone? And if she did succeed, how would she ever stand it?

six

"Happy Birthday, Mama!"

Megan barely opened one eye and squinted at her daughter. "Thank you, Baby." She scooted over and patted the bed beside her. "Why don't you snuggle up here with me, and we'll sleep just a little while longer?"

"No! I can't. I brought you a cup of coffee."

"Mmm. . .that's nice." Megan turned over and began to drift back into the delicious dream she'd been enjoying. A cup of coffee? She sat bolt upright in bed. "What?"

Sure enough, Sarah held a mug of brownish liquid. She offered it proudly to Megan. The coffee sloshed precariously, and Megan hurried to grab the cup before it spilled on the quilt. As she wrapped her hands around it, the first thing she noticed was the absence of heat. Her heart began to beat normally again. Whatever process Sarah had used to make this 'coffee,' at least it hadn't involved boiling water.

"Aren't you going to try it?"

"Yes, thank you so much, Sweetie. You're such a big girl." Megan cast another glance at the suspicious-looking mixture. "But first I need to run to the bathroom and get dressed." She set the cup on her nightstand.

"Okay, I'll just sit here and wait for you. Then you can try it when you get out."

Ten minutes later, Megan murmured a little prayer for protection and took a sip of Sarah's concoction. Forcing a smile, she chewed the gritty substance slowly and swallowed.

"I think I'll fix us some breakfast to go with this. Wouldn't want to drink it all up before I eat."

Sarah beamed and followed her to the kitchen. A large can of ground coffee sat on the counter. The lid lay beside it and black flecks were scattered around. So that was it. Instead of using the instant coffee, she'd pulled out the can and made Megan's birthday drink with ground coffee and tap water. Megan grimaced. She must have had to use a huge amount to make it dark with no hot water.

For the millionth time, she thanked God for blessing her with Sarah. How boring life would be without her. She'd thought her life would always be as empty as it had been right after Barry's death, but she'd been wrong.

Maybe she didn't look forward to birthdays like she had before, but that was just a fact of life. She couldn't help it that she no longer believed in happily-ever-afters. She'd always been intrigued by the way prisoners would make a mark on the wall for each day, month, or year. Her birthday served as a mental notch on the wall. She'd survived another year.

A peck on the kitchen door sent Sarah skipping to answer. Aunt Irene waved through the glass, her face wreathed in smiles. In her hand was a brightly wrapped package.

While Sarah was greeting the elderly woman, Megan hurried to dump the contents of her mug in the trash. She grinned when at least a half cup of grounds came out. A well-placed napkin hid the evidence. She rinsed the cup out and turned to welcome her neighbor.

"Happy Birthday!"

"Thank you. I can't believe you remembered."

"How could I forget? As soon as the month of May rolled around, Lola would start saying, 'It's almost time for Megan to get here, then it'll be her birthday.'"

"Yeah, Granny Lola always made a big deal out of it." Megan smiled at the happy memories.

"Speaking of that, I brought you a little something."

"Thanks." Megan took the package and tore into it. She knew it would be the only gift she received so she should make it last, but she couldn't.

The bright paper fell away to reveal a beautiful scrapbook with an elegantly hand stitched cover. Megan looked up at the tears in Aunt Irene's eyes. "Uh-oh. Are you going to make me cry on my birthday?"

Pictures of Megan and her grandmother lined the pages, punctuated by an occasional pebble, feather, or other keepsake, with the date and place it was found. Birthday napkins with a variety of dates proved Granny Lola's penchant toward making a big deal out of Megan's birthday. She was always keenly aware that by choosing to spend summers with her, her granddaughter was foregoing a family party, so she went overboard to compensate.

Megan flipped through the pages with wonder. Sarah clapped her hands at every new picture of her mama. When Megan started through the second time though, Sarah balked. "I'm going to go play." The little girl skipped down the hallway calling to her imaginary friends.

Megan squeezed Aunt Irene's hand. "How did you do this?"

"It wasn't easy. I had to resort to stealing and pray that the Lord would forgive me." The older woman absently pushed Megan's hair away from her face and looked into her eyes. "I knew where Lola kept this stuff, in an old shoebox up in the closet. Last time I stayed here with Sarah while you went to get supplies, I got it down and put it in my truck with this day in mind."

"Thank you."

"You always thank someone for stealing from you?"

A thought of Barry flashed across Megan's mind. If she did thank people for stealing from her, she'd have to thank her late husband, but she'd also have to thank Holt McFadden. . .for stealing her heart.

As if reading her mind, the elderly woman spoke. "You've had some company lately, haven't you?"

Relieved to have someone to talk to, Megan patted the chair beside her. Aunt Irene sat down and proved a captivated audience while Megan told her of her first meeting with Holt and everything in between up to present time.

Aunt Irene nodded. "I noticed that screen door was fixed when I pulled in the driveway. And the new clothesline post, as well. Those are mighty nice, but what about his heart?"

"What about his heart?"

"Is it good or bad?"

"Good." Megan bit back a grin. "Very, very good."

"Uh-oh, sounds like you've fallen pretty hard."

The grin faded. "Well, you know I can't really. I mean he's a senator. Can you imagine how that would look?" She held up her hand to stop the protest she knew was coming. "Even if we could get beyond that, don't you figure senators' families have to get out occasionally?"

"I reckon senators' families are the same as everybody else. Besides, I've told you a hundred times. It wouldn't hurt you to get out more. You haven't done anything wrong, yet you hide out here like you're ashamed."

"I just don't want to cause the people I love any more pain."

"Maybe you need to stop thinking you are so powerful, Megan Girl. You didn't cause anyone pain."

Megan shook her head. "Arguing with you is like arguing

with a stump and about as profitable, so I'll say no more."

"Good! Because I'm about to fix you a breakfast so delicious you won't have time to talk. That's the rest of my birthday present for you." She pointed to a grocery bag beside her chair that Megan hadn't noticed. "I brought the fixins for ham and mushroom omelets."

"Oh, that sounds wonderful." Megan realized she still had little pieces of ground coffee in her mouth. One of Aunt Irene's famous omelets would get rid of that.

"Now, you just go and relax while I fix breakfast. Then, after you've eaten, I want you to get out and do whatever you want for the next few hours. I'm taking care of things in here."

Megan smiled. Last night as she'd lain in bed, she'd suddenly known what she wanted to do for her birthday. "Thanks," she said and dropped a kiss on the top of Aunt Irene's head.

"That sewing room's off limit too," her neighbor called as Megan started down the hallway.

"Come see for yourself what I have in mind and you won't say that," Megan teased.

She slipped into the sewing room and quickly found the material that had filled her dreams last night. United States flags danced across the fabric in patriotic celebration.

"You're going to make a patriotic quilt for your birthday?" Aunt Irene asked from the doorway. "And this has you in a good mood?" She shook her head. "Sometimes you worry me, Megan Watson."

"Don't worry. I'll explain it to you." Megan eased up off her knees, the red, white, and blue material still in her hands. "My whole life is governed by what I can't do. I can't draw attention to myself. I can't be a part of my parents' lives without bringing additional shame to them. And most of all, right now, I can't have a relationship with Senator Holt McFadden because it would ruin his career. So for my birthday, I decided to do something I can do."

"Make a quilt?"

"Yes. For Holt." She smiled. "He mentioned that he didn't have any, not even a lap quilt. He's done so many nice things for me, and all I've been able to give him in return is grief."

"Uh-huh." Aunt Irene's expression was doubtful. "How are you going to explain this gift without giving him the idea that you're open to more than friendship?"

"That's the beauty of it. I'm not going to send the quilt until the fall or early winter. By then he will have forgotten all about me, and my own feelings won't be so strong, either." She ignored Aunt Irene's raised eyebrow. "I can write a nicely-worded note thanking him for helping us out this summer. And I will always know he has something to remember me by. . ." Her words stuck in her throat like glue. Instead of the peace she'd envisioned after deciding on the gift last night, a fist-sized knot seemed to have moved in where her stomach used to be.

"Megan, I wish you could give yourself a break for once."

She nodded. "I know, but I can't."

"Well. . . ," Aunt Irene crossed her arms, ". . .if you're determined to be a martyr, I can at least be sure you don't starve. I'm going to go fix breakfast."

As soon as she was alone, Megan ran her hand over the fabric. She'd cut out the individual squares as soon as she'd bought it so it was ready to put together. She held the print against the bolts of solid-colored material and finally settled on navy blue for the strips between the squares.

That would be perfect for the back, as well. Navy was a masculine color, and Holt McFadden was nothing if not masculine.

seven

A bright pink daisy brushed against the corner of Holt's mouth, and he blew gently to see if he could reposition it without crushing it. It refused to budge so he leaned a little farther to the right and peered around the huge bouquet of flowers. He held the cut crystal vase in his left hand and gripped the steering wheel tightly with his right. He hadn't wanted to set the bouquet down, because he was afraid it would turn over, so he'd driven all the way from town with a strong floral scent wafting up his nose.

Breathing a sigh of relief at the sight of Megan's mailbox, he turned right and killed the motor, thankful that her driveway had a bit of a downhill slope. The truck coasted to a silent stop. He gingerly opened the door and gathered the birthday cake in his free hand. There was no way he could get everything else. He'd have to make two trips up to the porch and hope he wasn't discovered.

❧

Megan straightened and looked at the clock. Aunt Irene had been gone for six hours. They'd shared a delicious breakfast and the older lady had slipped out, leaving Megan eagerly working on the lap quilt. She'd stopped for five minutes to fix Sarah a sandwich for lunch but had decided not to take time to eat. For some reason she couldn't explain, today seemed to scream freedom, and she was afraid tomorrow she'd be back to doubting everything, even giving this quilt to Holt. Therefore, it was urgent that she finish today.

And she finally had. She took it gingerly off the rack and hemmed it on her sewing machine. When it was completed, she laid it out and stood back to admire her creation. Holt would love it. Her heart dropped. Not that she'd see his eyes light up when he opened it.

A knock on the door interrupted her thoughts. Had Aunt Irene forgotten something or come back to fix supper? She quickly folded the quilt and set it on the shelf, then hurried to answer the door.

Just as she reached the living room, Sarah yelled, "Mr. Holt!" and threw the door open.

Megan froze in her steps as she stared at Holt sharing the doorway with the biggest bouquet of spring flowers she'd ever seen. "Holt!"

"Happy Birthday," he said, with a sheepish grin.

Her legs trembling, Megan crossed over to take the vase from his hands. "Come on in."

"Okay." But instead of entering the house, he turned toward the rocker and swung back around with a cake in his hands.

"Happy Birthday Megan!" was spelled out in bright red icing and the entire cake was covered in flowers that had obviously been color-coordinated with the bouquet. Megan's head was buzzing, and for a moment, she thought she was going to pass right out on the floor. That would be a funny way of showing her appreciation. "You shouldn't have."

"I shouldn't have?" He grinned and set the cake on the small round table in the corner. "I think I should have."

"Thanks."

"Save your thanks until you see the last gift. You may hate it."

"There's more?" she asked weakly, sinking into a chair by the door as Holt went outside again.

Seconds later, he came in toting what appeared to be a rolled up rug. He marched past her down the hallway with Sarah skipping at his heels. Megan couldn't contain her curiosity when he entered her sewing room. She had to go see what it was.

She was thankful for her habit of folding quilts wrong side out. Even if he noticed the new lap quilt on the shelf, all he would see was navy blue material. She poked her head cautiously into the room, just as Holt unrolled his bundle with a flourish.

A beautiful plush runner with a print that exactly matched the multicolored room stretched the length of the previously bare floor in front of her machine. Sarah immediately began to do forward rolls up and down from one end to the other.

"Oh, Holt, I can't believe you thought of that." She pressed her hand to her back. "I always intended to get something to stand on there, but I just never got around to it."

"Well, my chiropractor will tell you that you need some cushion under your feet when you're on them all day like you are." He offered a rueful grin. "I'm nothing if not practical."

"Oh, really? Where's the practicality in those flowers in there?" Megan's heart thudded. What had he been thinking?

"Well, I guess if you got hungry enough you could eat them." He sounded so serious she giggled. "Or you could dry them and maybe some of them would make healing herbs."

"Healing herbs? From a florist's bouquet? You're reaching."

"Would you believe they were on the clearance shelf, so I just grabbed them as an afterthought?"

I might have if it weren't for the color-coordinated cake. "That explains it then. You really like a bargain, don't you? Guess I should be glad they didn't have lunch meat on clearance, or I probably would have gotten a pound of that for my birthday."

"Actually. . .there was some liverwurst on sale. It was a tough call between the flowers and that." He feigned a look of great concern. "Hope I made the right decision."

She playfully slugged him on the arm. "Definitely, and just to show you I mean it, how about I fix us some coffee to go with that cake?"

"You're a woman after my own heart," Holt said, as they walked down the hall.

Megan didn't know what to say. She couldn't exactly say, "No, not really. I'm trying to protect your heart from me." So she just remained silent.

While Megan went into make the coffee, Holt sat down in the living room.

"Whose scrapbook?"

"That's mine."

"May I look at it?"

"Sure."

Her hands trembled as she measured the coffee into the pot and poured the water in. The pictures in that book were like a photograph story of her life. It was as if she were baring her soul to him, and she wasn't even in the same room.

She heard Sarah, then Holt's deep voice rumbled, but she couldn't make out what they were saying. Sarah was probably filling in the narrative for the pictures. She'd made Megan tell her about each one earlier, and she had a very good memory.

She stuck her head in the living room. "Holt, do you want sugar and cream?"

Sarah and Holt both jumped, then laughed. They were wearing party hats and had noisemakers. After their chuckle, they began to blow the little horns as if it were midnight on New Year's Eve. Sarah hurried over with a hat for Megan. Not wanting to disappoint her daughter, Megan bent down and allowed the four year old to put it carefully on her head. She smiled.

Holt stood and winked at Sarah, who was practically jumping with excitement. "I'll fix my own coffee. You just have a seat in here with Sarah."

Megan obediently sat down, and Holt made his way into the kitchen as if he was very much at home in the little house. She heard him opening drawers. "Do you need some help?"

"No, no, I've got it. You just relax."

She nodded absently. Everything had happened so fast. She couldn't believe she'd gone from spending her birthday alone with Sarah to having this elaborate party for three.

"Sarah? I'm ready." Holt's voice called from the kitchen.

"Okay," Sarah answered and leaped to her feet. She scurried to the light switch and turned it off. "Ready!"

Megan watched in disbelief as the kitchen door came open, and Holt walked out carrying her cake, ablaze with candles. "Happy Birthday to you. . ." Neither Holt nor Sarah were particularly on key, but Megan knew she'd never hear a sweeter rendition of that particular song as long as she lived.

❧

Later, after Sarah was tucked into bed, Megan and Holt relaxed in the front porch rockers. As they looked up at the seemingly innumerable stars and the smell of honeysuckle filled the air, Megan sighed.

"This has been the best birthday ever."

"Really?" Holt's voice sounded doubtful. "I saw that scrapbook. I had some pretty tough competition."

Megan chuckled. "Yeah, you did. Granny Lola sure knew how to celebrate. These last three birthdays without her have been awful." She paused, struggling for the right words, listening to the chirping crickets. "What you did today helped to erase those bad birthday memories and bring back the joy Granny put into celebrating. I'll be forever grateful."

"Hmm. . .eternal gratitude? Surely a good politician could think of a way to turn that to his advantage?"

She swallowed the lump in her throat, thankful for his way of lightening a heavy situation. "Hey, I fixed supper for you. What more did you want?"

"Oh, I don't know. Maybe a night out on the town sometime? Supper and a movie?" He cleared his throat, and she found his obvious nervousness—so out of place in this confident man—endearing. "Don't get me wrong. I love the farm, but I just thought maybe Friday night you could get a sitter—"

"No, I can't."

"Well, in that case, maybe there's a kid's movie playing. I love being with Sarah. We could all go together."

She was so glad this conversation was taking place in pitch dark, otherwise, her expression would definitely give her away. "I appreciate the offer, Holt. But I just don't think it's a good idea." She knew she should just tell him why, but letting him go by means of noble sacrifice seemed infinitely preferable to losing him due to his disdain of her past.

He abruptly stood. "Well, okay, then. Thanks for allowing me to share today, Megan."

She pushed to her feet as well. She couldn't see his face, but she knew he was aggravated with her constant rebuffs. Her shoulders sagged. That was kind of the point, wasn't it?

"Thank you." She cringed lest her husky voice betray her emotions, but he didn't seem to notice.

"Good night." He reached for her hand, and against her better judgment, she took it. He pulled her nearer and dropped a light kiss on her forehead. Her legs trembled, and she thought her heart would beat right out of her chest.

"Good night." She stood and watched the shadowy figure of the best man she'd ever known fade into the inky blackness. Only when his truck motor started did she go inside to face a sleepless night.

eight

It had been a month since Megan's birthday. Holt had gotten into the habit of stopping by the farm on Tuesday and Thursday afternoons, doing a few odd jobs, and enjoying the sunset with the two Watson females. Often—as he had today—he brought Chinese food for supper. It was Megan's favorite, and he was hoping that the old adage about the way to a man's heart being through his stomach worked in reverse too.

Little Sarah had warmed to him quickly, but Megan was another story. Their friendship had seemed to be on the verge of progressing to a new level the day of her birthday, but if anything, it had gone backwards from that day, as if a wall had been constructed between them.

Until today, that is, Holt thought as his pickup bounced along the gravel road. Today, he was going to make a brave attempt at scaling the invisible wall and ask Megan to the family Fourth of July picnic.

Holt's brother, Cade, had married last December, and like all happy newlyweds, he felt sorry for anyone who didn't have what he shared with his new wife, Annalisa. The couple was hosting the annual gathering at the Circle M, and Cade had called last night to remind Holt and be sure he was coming.

No matter how hard his older brother tried, he couldn't hide his concern that Holt might not be over his breakup with his old girlfriend. Nor could Cade conceal his joy when Holt had assured him that he'd be there with a guest.

Now it was up to Holt to produce one.

There was only one person he wanted to take to the picnic. Two, actually, counting Sarah. He'd asked Megan out before, but she'd always had a convenient excuse. She seemed so happy to be with him that he was beginning to wonder if she was afraid to leave her little house in the hills.

He was convinced his dream to someday serve as governor was from God—a way for Him to use Holt for His good. What would the people of Arkansas think of a First Lady who refused to leave the farm? He pushed his discomfort aside. Surely God wouldn't bring Megan into his life, only to make him choose between her and his career.

❧

Megan forked another piece of Almond Fried Chicken. "You have to stop this," she groaned. "I'll be bigger than a house by the Fourth of July if you don't."

"Aw, Meg, it's not so bad. We always go for a walk afterwards. You probably burn off all the extra calories."

"Huh! Remind me not to let you be my diet counselor." She grinned at his hurt little boy look.

"Speaking of the Fourth of July. . ."

"Yeah?"

"Do you have plans?"

"Hmm. . .quilt?"

"That doesn't sound like very much fun."

"What are you going to do?" She hated to ask. She felt sure his celebration would involve large crowds, red, white, and blue banners, and speeches. She was equally sure he was about to ask her to attend. Then there would be no choice but to tell him the truth.

"My folks have an annual family thing. The location rotates around from house to house, but the food's always delicious and the company's always good."

"Somehow, that's not what I envisioned you doing on a patriotic holiday."

He nodded. "One year, I skipped it because I thought I had to attend a political rally. The only thing I could think about was my brothers eating all the barbecue without me. I flubbed my whole speech. After that, I decided I'd stick with the McFaddens on holidays and save the campaigning for the rest of the year."

"What a great idea."

"I'm glad to hear you say that, because I want you and Sarah to come with me this year."

She opened her mouth, but the words wouldn't come. Now was the time to tell him why they couldn't ever be more than friends and why she definitely couldn't go with him to the picnic. Instead, she shoved another bite of chicken in her mouth and gave a noncommittal shrug. The small bite seemed to grow bigger and bigger. When she finally swallowed, he was still looking at her, apparently waiting for an answer.

She couldn't help but be impressed with how much his family meant to him. Every time they were together, he managed to knock another chip off her preconceived image of a smooth politician. Maybe that was why she was finding it harder and harder to avoid growing close to him.

"We can't."

"Why?"

"I can't leave Aunt Irene alone that long."

"Your aunt lives with you?" Holt looked around the room as if expecting a previously unnoticed old lady to materialize in a corner.

"No, and she's not really my aunt. She was my grand-mother's nearest neighbor, and now she's mine. I check on her every day."

"Is she sick?"

"No," Megan said, feeling defensive, "but she's elderly, and I don't want anything to happen to her."

"So she's active?"

"Yes."

"Then why can't she come too? The more the merrier." Holt sat back in his chair and fixed her with a level gaze.

He wasn't going to make this easy for her.

Then again, she didn't owe him anything. They'd had some nice times together, but she still had the right to say no to an invitation.

"No, thanks. Maybe next time." Why had she added that last? Next time he asked, if there was a next time, which she doubted after this, she'd have to tell him the real reason she couldn't date him.

He pushed abruptly to his feet. "I'd better be going."

Logically, she knew the best thing she could do would be to let him go, but her heart nudged her to stop him. She stood. "Without our walk? I can see those calories jumping for glee that they aren't going to be burned tonight after all."

Her silliness elicited a small grin that quickly disappeared. Then he stared at her so long she wanted to avert her eyes. "Have it your way. Let's walk."

ᴥ

The two adults walked in silence, but Sarah kept up an imaginative chatter that filled in the conversational void. "Luuuuucy!!!" she called, then she glanced back at Megan and Holt. "Lucy's run off again." She stopped walking suddenly and fixed Holt with an inquisitive stare. "Do you know who Lucy is?"

Megan bit back a grin. There was little doubt that Holt did know who Lucy was—although Sarah had a wide repertoire of imaginary playmates. He wouldn't admit to his knowledge though, because they both loved to hear Sarah say "imaginary."

Holt shook his head.

"She's my 'may-nay' friend."

He nodded solemnly.

When Sarah turned to skip on down the path in search of Lucy, Holt met Megan's grin with one of his own. She hoped that meant he'd come to terms with her refusal of his invitation. Surely he realized friendship was all she had to offer.

❧

Four days later, Megan guided the red laser light along the familiar quilting pattern. As she watched the simple strand of ivy take shape on the fabric, she wished she were doing a difficult pattern, instead. Then her mind wouldn't have time to dwell on the fact that she hadn't heard from Holt since Tuesday night.

She realized now she'd been overly optimistic to assume that a shared grin over Sarah had signaled his acceptance of her decision. He had only said a few more words that night before leaving, and she'd noticed there had been no promise of future visits.

She'd spent the past four days reminding herself she should be happy to have accomplished her goal of breaking things off with Holt. Her hermit-like attitude had won the battle for her without her even having to try. But her heart proclaimed it a hollow victory.

The jangling of the phone startled her.

Sarah ran into the room. "Mama, the phone is ringing."

Megan had to smile at the four yearold's propensity for stating the obvious. She stopped the needle where it was and grabbed the cordless phone beside her.

"Hello?"

"Hi, Megan. It's Holt."

Her heart thudded so loudly she was afraid he'd hear it over the line. "Hi."

"I'm sorry I didn't make it Thursday. I got tied up in Little Rock and just got home."

"Don't they have phones in Little Rock?" As soon as the words were out, she wished them back. He didn't have to call. They hadn't had a date.

"Yes, Meg," he responded with the teasing tone she was coming to know so well, "they have phones in Little Rock." She could see his grin as clearly as if he were standing in front of her. "I forgot to take your number with me. You—being such a social person—may not realize this, but it's unlisted."

"Oh." Her face grew hot.

"I thought you might want to go out to lunch with me after church tomorrow." He paused, but before she could speak, he continued. "You and Sarah. And, of course, Aunt Irene."

Megan wracked her brain for an excuse. It had been on the tip of her tongue to tell him that Aunt Irene ate Sunday lunch with them, but he'd apparently already thought of that. "What time do you get out of church?"

"We get out at twelve, but I thought I might go with you. Since I've moved, the church you go to is much closer than the one I grew up in, and I've been wanting to visit there anyway. Plus, that way we'd be ready to go eat when it was over."

"Where would we eat?" If quilting ever failed, she could become a reporter, she thought. She had at least two of the five Ws down pat.

"Well, The Fish House is what I had in mind, but not everyone likes fish. . ."

"I love it. It used to be my favorite place to eat around here, but I haven't been there in years." That had sounded suspiciously like she was accepting.

"What about Sarah? Will it be okay with her?"

Sarah had never eaten in a restaurant. It probably wouldn't matter what they were serving, she'd be thrilled. But Megan wasn't about to pass on that ammunition to Mr. "you need to get out more" McFadden.

"Sure, she loves fish."

"Is that a yes?"

She hesitated. The relief of hearing his voice again was still coursing through her. It was only lunch. "Yes, Holt, that's a yes."

"Great. I'll see you then."

Megan hung up and walked back to her quilting machine. It was amazing how much lighter her heart felt. She sewed for a few minutes in total peace. Then the voice of reason prevailed. What would happen when he found out about her past?

❧

Father, I need your help. I don't know what to do. You already know my feelings for Megan are growing daily. She can't let go of the past, though, and because of that, I'm confused about the future. And even if I do get her to come back out into the world, I'm afraid I'll let her down. Holt cleared his throat and gritted his teeth. *If I can't be strong enough to stand by her no matter what happens, then don't let her care for me as I do her. If it's not Your will for me to be with Megan, please make it plain to me. Your will be done. In Jesus' name, amen.*

Holt stood and picked up his Bible. He had offered Megan a ride to church, but since the building was between his house and hers, she'd insisted on driving. He wondered if she'd take her own vehicle to the restaurant as well.

As he drove the short distance, he thought about the prayer he'd just prayed. He'd long ago learned the importance of wanting God's will over his own, but lately, with Marshall's pressure, he sometimes wondered how far he would go to help God along with His plans for Holt's career. And now, asking for God's will in his relationship with Megan had been more difficult than he'd imagined.

nine

Megan couldn't believe God's timing. Holt sat on one side of her and Aunt Irene on the other as the Bible Class teacher read aloud from chapter five of Matthew. "You are the light of the world. A city on a hill cannot be hidden. Neither do people light a light a lamp and put it under a bowl. Instead they put it on its stand, and it gives light to everyone in the house. In the same way, let your light shine before men, that they may see your good deeds and praise your Father in heaven."

Aunt Irene nodded vigorously, and Megan knew her neighbor was thinking of all the times she had quoted that verse to Megan concerning her hiding. Holt looked at the older woman then caught Megan's eye and nodded slightly. Though he hadn't quoted scripture to her, at least twice that Megan could remember he'd referred to this very passage in reference to her hermit-hood, as he jokingly called it.

Was she guilty of hiding her light? Maybe. But then again, maybe she felt she would do more damage as a Christian example by going out in public and reminding people of the past.

No, if she were honest, she had to admit that her reasons for seclusion were purely selfish. She'd had enough humiliation and reproach to last a lifetime. She shook her head as if to refute the two nodders flanking her, but in reality, she was trying to shake away the memory of the humiliation and reproach Jesus had suffered for His purpose.

Tears obscured her vision, and she searched discreetly in her purse for a tissue. Agreeing to go to lunch with Holt had been a mistake. Except for loving Sarah and Aunt Irene, she'd effectively closed the door on her feelings three years ago. Now that he'd convinced her to open it, even a crack, she was a bundle of emotion.

◆

Megan was coming around. Holt had noticed her tears in church this morning, and he knew God was softening her heart. Now, if He would thicken Holt's skin so that he could be the protector she so obviously needed. As strong as his growing feelings for her had become, he thought he could face down a fire-breathing dragon on her behalf, but how could he be sure?

Meeting Aunt Irene had proven to be pure fun. The elderly woman cracked jokes and teased in a way that made Holt feel right at home. He reached to pull her chair out for her as they gathered around the table at the restaurant.

"Megan, your young man is trying to pull my chair out from under me. Can't you control him?"

Megan colored to a rosy pink. " 'Fraid not."

Holt leaned in toward her as he helped her get seated. "Does that mean I am your young man?" he whispered.

She tossed her hair down over her shoulder so that it hung like a curtain blocking her face from his view. She picked up the menu and appeared to be studying the choices intently.

When the waitress brought a booster chair, Sarah clapped her hands together in delight.

"Do you get this excited every time you use a booster chair?" Holt teased.

"I've never used a. . .um. . .rooster chair," Sarah proclaimed.

"Look, Honey." Megan directed Sarah's attention to the kid's menu. "Let's look at the pictures and pick out what you want to eat."

Sarah's eyes grew wide. "You mean they'll fix whatever I want?"

Suddenly, it hit Holt. He teased Megan about being a hermit, but she truly was. If he were a betting man, he'd bet her daughter had never been inside a restaurant before. Getting Megan to come out of her shell might be harder than he'd thought.

"Senator McFadden! How have you been?"

Holt looked up at Josiah Barclay, then rose to his feet.

"I'm fine, Josiah. How are you?" He couldn't believe the Barclays were here. He was seeing them more often than he was his own mom and dad lately.

"Fine, fine." The big man nodded repeatedly and peered at Holt's dining companions. Holt noticed Josiah's wife had joined him and was following his curious gaze with one of her own.

"Hello, Barbara."

She nodded. "Senator." The woman gave her husband a barely perceptible nudge with her elbow.

"So, Senator, is this some of your family?" He motioned toward Megan who was as white as the tablecloth.

Holt wanted to guard Megan from any speculation, but if he didn't introduce her, he was afraid she'd think it was because of his concern about public opinion.

He indicated Aunt Irene with his hand, smiling at the woman who looked like she'd do anything to help Megan. "You probably know Mrs. Irene Hanley. Beside her are Megan Watson and her daughter, Sarah. They're all three neighbors of mine.

"Ladies, this is Josiah and Barbara Barclay. You may know them. They own Barclay's Hardware here in town."

"Mrs. Irene, it's been awhile since we've seen you."

"I don't get out much these days. Just to buy groceries mostly." Aunt Irene's voice seemed stilted, and Holt knew she was nervous on Megan's behalf. No doubt she knew the Barclays' reputation for gossip.

Instead of responding to Aunt Irene, Barbara narrowed her eyes. "Of course. Megan Watson. Lola's granddaughter."

ᴈ

Why had she let Holt talk her into coming out into public? Megan nodded politely as if she thought Barbara's accusation was a greeting, and as if she weren't about to pass out from terror. If she'd had any doubts about her life choices, the gleam in Barbara Barclay's eyes had washed them away.

"Let's see, Megan, you're living in Lola's house now, aren't you?"

Megan nodded again.

Barbara turned to Holt as if just struck by a sudden thought. "That's not far at all from where you live, is it, Senator?"

If Megan hadn't come to know Holt so well in the past month, she wouldn't have recognized the flicker of extreme distaste and irritation that passed across his face. "No, Ma'am, it isn't. That's why I said they were my 'neighbors.'"

In spite of her terror, Megan giggled at his unexpected subtle sarcasm. She tried to turn it into a cough, but in spite of her best efforts, it remained a renegade giggle. She covered her mouth with the large white napkin. "Excuse me."

Since this unacceptable behavior showed no sign of stopping, she rose to her feet and hurried to the rest room. As soon as the door closed behind her, she leaned against the counter, helpless to stop the laughter. Stress. Before Barry, she'd always giggled when the stress got to be too much. She never giggled at any other time, but give her a big dose of stress and her tickle box just automatically turned over.

She perched on the edge of the marble top double vanity. After a few minutes, the laughter stopped as abruptly as it had started. Just as quickly, tears filled her eyes. She snagged a tissue from the handy slot between the sinks.

Why was she here? She'd come mostly to prove to Holt that she wasn't a "hermit." But she was. She grabbed another tissue. She belonged at the farm with her quilting machine and Sarah and. . .Holt. Only he didn't belong at the farm at all. He belonged here. . .where the people were.

She didn't know how long she stayed in the bathroom. She had been in such a hurry to get away from the table that she hadn't brought her purse, so she had no way to freshen up. All she could do was splash some cold water on her puffy eyes and red face and hope for the best.

When she reached the table, the Barclays were no longer around and everyone pretended things were normal. *Quite a stretch,* thought Megan, *to pretend I'm normal.*

"We told them what we wanted to drink, Mama. I told them you drink tea." Sarah bounced up and down in her booster chair. "Look she's bringing it on a tray."

"Neat, isn't it?" Megan was immeasurably grateful for Sarah's distraction.

The waitress set the tray full of drinks down and sorted them out. When she flipped open her order pad, Sarah gasped. "Just like on TV."

"What would you like to eat, Little Lady?" the waitress asked Sarah.

"I'll take this." She pointed at the picture of the child's fish plate. "And this. And this. And this." Her little finger flew from one food picture to the other.

Megan felt Holt's grin, but she just couldn't look him in the eye. He must think she was a terrible mother on top of being a blithering idiot. "Sarah. You can't have one of everything. Let's try the catfish."

Sarah considered her for a moment, then grinned. "Okay. And some French-fries. And a chocolate shake."

Megan stared at the tiny girl. "You'll never eat all of that, Honey."

"Please." Sarah offered Megan the pleading look she saved for special requests.

Why not? This may be the only time she gets to eat out until she's old enough to go on her own. I'm certainly not leaving the farm again any time soon. "Okay." Megan nodded to the waitress. "Fish plate and a chocolate shake for her, and I'll have the same."

When the waitress had gone with their orders, Holt smiled. "They're gone." He spoke softly.

"There are more where they came from," she muttered. She finally met his gaze. "You have no idea."

"I do have an idea. I've had my share of dealing with people like that." Holt's voice was gentle. "When I was campaigning, I'd hear so many rumors about myself, I considered voting for the other guy."

Aunt Irene snickered, and Megan couldn't keep from smiling.

"But then, when the polls were closed, it turned out the large majority of the public recognized the big talkers for what they were. It's that way in real life too."

Megan stared at him. Did he know her secret? Or was this just a generic reassurance for a hermit? She'd always known there was the possibility he would remember Barry's case from the media coverage and connect it with her. She'd even tried to prepare her heart for the eventuality. But she'd always assumed as soon as he found out about her past, he'd stop coming around.

❧

On the trip back home after lunch, Megan insisted Aunt Irene ride in the front seat with Holt while she kept Sarah company in the back. The more distance she could put between herself and Holt, the better off she'd be. Just by agreeing to lunch, she knew she'd been asking for trouble.

She had to end their relationship today. If he did know about her past, which she couldn't believe, he was not reacting rationally. Why would he have pushed her to be seen with him in public?

If he didn't know, then she was taking the chance of causing irreparable harm to his career just by allowing him to be seen with her. Either way, she wouldn't be going out again, and he wouldn't be satisfied with that for long, no matter how much he gently teased her about being a hermit.

She dreaded facing his persuasiveness. Barry had oozed it, and if she hadn't been so naïve that would have been a warning. Holt was even smoother than Barry was, but she found herself believing his charm was genuine.

Apparently, Aunt Irene did too. Though she'd never said much, she hadn't liked Barry, but it was obvious from the looks she was giving Megan that Holt had her total approval.

"Do you play dominoes?" Aunt Irene's abrupt question affirmed Megan's thoughts.

"I used to play with my brothers when we were growing up. But I haven't in years." Holt smiled, but puzzlement was evident on his face.

"Let's go back to my house and play dominoes. It's what we do after lunch on Sundays. You can take us to church services tonight, and Megan can pick up her van then." The older lady's inclusion of him in the family was obvious, not to mention her desire for him to stay around. Megan felt the heat creep up her cheeks again. She was going to have to have a talk with Aunt Irene.

"That sounds like a wonderful idea." He paused and turned his attention to Megan. "Is that okay with you?" As his gaze met hers in the rearview mirror, she felt as if he could read her thoughts. Instead of the normal teasing glint in his eyes, there was sympathy. Somehow, he understood she was reluctant and hated for her to be pushed into spending time with him.

"Sure, that would be fun." Her heart constricted as the smile lit up his face. She'd meant to say no, but the kindness in his expression had been her undoing.

Two hours later, even though Megan was enjoying herself, she wished she'd gone with her first instinct. After a game of friendly dominoes, Aunt Irene commandeered Sarah to help her make cookies.

"Oh, Megan," the elderly woman called as she walked into the kitchen, "do you think Holt would help you hang those blinds we've been meaning to get up in the living room?"

Megan bit back the urge to follow her neighbor into the kitchen and leave Holt to his own devices. She was definitely going to have a talk with Aunt Irene. Matchmaking had always been a hobby for the older woman, but she knew Megan wasn't in the market for a man, especially not Holt.

After the kitchen door slammed behind the cookie makers, silence stretched out in the living room like a heavy rug. Holt's gaze bore into her, and she felt again as if he were examining her inner thoughts. She was growing used to his mixture of serious observation and silly humor, so it didn't surprise her when he spoke.

"Well, Private Watson, you heard the General. Let's get that blind hung. We've got church in two hours." He pushed to his feet, shoulders back and feet together. "Ten-hut!"

Megan couldn't resist. She stood quickly and tilting her head back to where he still towered above her, she offered a sharp salute. "Yes, SIR!"

They laughed, and she retrieved the blind from the front closet, along with a small toolbox.

"Do you take care of her maintenance by yourself usually?"

"We do it together. She may want to appear helpless today because it suits her purpose." Megan grinned. "But she's still pretty handy with a screwdriver or even a paintbrush."

"Her purpose?" The teasing note in Holt's voice proved he had no doubt what Megan was referring to. "What would that be?"

Megan offered an unladylike snort. "Are you going to stand on the stool? Or do you want me to?"

"Are you sure you'd be tall enough, even if you did climb up on the stool?" He held his hand out in the air as if measuring her height and finding her definitely lacking. "I think I'd better do it."

Megan glared at his mischievous grin. How dare he insinuate she was short, just because he was a first cousin to the Jolly Green Giant? "Don't tell me. Let me guess. You probably took that class about winning friends and influencing people before you ran for the senate, didn't you? That's why you're so smooth."

"So. . . ," Holt climbed up on the stool. He looked down at her and arched one eyebrow. "You don't think I'm very good at winning friends? I can't be all bad. You've been spending time with me this summer." Suddenly, he shook the stool with his feet, and she grabbed it. He grinned. "And you were willing to catch me if I fell just then, weren't you?"

Megan stared into his sparkling eyes. In spite of her sarcastic comment, Holt McFadden was undoubtedly good at winning friends, but he was a champion at winning hearts, if hers was any indication. "I would have done that for anybody."

"Ouch." Holt flinched as if she'd hit him, but she noticed a grin edged at the corners of his mouth as he turned back to the job at hand. He soon had the blind neatly covering the previously bare window. He stepped down off the stool and stumbled as his feet hit the hardwood floor. Teasingly, he flung his arms around Megan. "Whew. Thanks for saving me."

"Yeah, right." She hoped he couldn't hear her heart hammering against her ribcage. She knew he was joking, but he hadn't released her.

"Megan." His face was only inches from hers.

Their gazes locked, and she braced herself for the kiss she knew was coming. It felt so hard to catch her breath.

She was falling in love with Holt McFadden.

"No!" With both hands, she shoved his chest and disentangled herself from his embrace. "No." Her legs trembled, but she stomped quickly to the front door and hurried outside.

❧

Holt sank down on the stool he'd been standing on minutes before. How did she do it? How did she drive him absolutely crazy? Every time they seemed to be growing close, she pulled back as if he was a nightmare suddenly come to life. The horror on her face just now had been palpable.

"Hi, Mr. Holt!" Sarah trotted into the room. In spite of his churning emotions, Holt smiled at the tiny sprite in the oversized apron. Her face was liberally sprinkled with flour. A few suspicious brown smudges suggested she'd been sampling the chocolate chips. She held up her arms, and he automatically lifted her onto his lap. "Where's Mama?"

"She's outside." Holt didn't have a clue what explanation to offer, but apparently none was necessary.

Sarah slid to the floor. "She's probably playing with the puppies then." She quickly disappeared out the door.

Holt tried to decide whether his presence outside would be a help or a hindrance when Sarah burst back in.

"Aunt Irene! Mama's crying!" Tears were evident in the little girl's eyes, and her excited voice brought the elderly woman running from the kitchen.

"What is it, Sarah?"

"Mama's—"

The front door opened, and Megan entered the room. "Sarah." Her eyes were red, but there were no tears. She held her arms out to the little girl. "Come here." Sarah's troubled expression cleared. She hurried to be enfolded in her mother's hug.

While the mother and daughter embraced, Holt met Aunt Irene's gaze. The woman was shaking her head.

"Who wants a cookie?" Aunt Irene asked.

"I do!" Sarah grabbed Megan by the hand. "Come on, Mama. I made them myself!"

"Holt, won't you join us for a cookie?" Though Megan didn't look at him, her voice held an unspoken apology he heard loud and clear.

Holt nodded. Whatever was going on between them would have to be addressed, but now was not the time. As they trooped into the kitchen, he knew it would take more than a cookie to work things out between them.

☙

Megan closed her van door, then glanced back to where Holt's truck had just pulled in behind her. It looked like she'd get the chance to have that talk with him tonight, after all. They hadn't spoken privately anymore at Aunt Irene's, and she'd left him talking to some men after church.

She had assumed he'd head back to his house after they'd said good-bye. If she'd known he was going to follow her home, she'd have kept Sarah with her instead of letting her stay at Aunt Irene's for awhile when she dropped the older woman off.

It was probably just as well, Megan thought. Especially after Sarah saw her tears this afternoon, she would undoubtedly be more upset if she overheard Megan telling Holt not to come over anymore.

"Hey." He'd covered the distance between their vehicles with a few long strides.

"I thought you were going home."

He nodded toward the rockers on the porch. "Can we sit?"

"Sure." She followed him up to the porch where he stood hesitantly waiting for her to sit first. "What?! You're not going to pull my rocker out for me?"

He looked confused for a second, then his expression cleared. "Why, Megan. I believe that was a joke."

"You think? Uh-oh. You must be rubbing off on me." She sat down. When he folded himself into the corresponding chair, she met his gaze. "So, what did you come back for?"

Now why had she said that? She was supposed to jump right into her good-bye speech.

"I wanted to talk for a few minutes." He cleared his throat and stared out across the yard to the barn. She followed his

gaze. The sun was setting, and once again, they were sharing the beautiful scene. It seemed to have become their
hallmark – watching sunsets together. One ending after
another. He turned back toward her. "I was hoping you'd
reconsider about the Fourth of July picnic. You'd really
enjoy it. You deserve to get out and have some fun." He
hesitated for a second. "So does Sarah."

Megan gasped. "Oh, that's low, McFadden, really low.
Using a preschooler to get a date." She hated the direction
this conversation was going, but she seemed helpless to stop
her harsh words. How dare he bring her daughter into this?

"But she's really not a preschooler, is she?" His voice was
soft. "Because that implies she goes to preschool, and except
for church and an occasional outing to Aunt Irene's, Sarah
never leaves the farm, does she?"

His tone was calm, but the accusation in his words propelled Megan to her feet. "Sarah has a good life." Suddenly,
her legs gave way. She sank back down into the rocker and
covered her face with her hands.

"I can't do this. You have no idea who I am." Suddenly,
Megan remembered the series of phone calls she'd received
during that awful time after Barry's death. The unidentified
caller's words echoed in her ears. *Who are you?* "Maybe I don't
even know who I am anymore."

"Maybe I know you better than you think." His big hand
covered hers, warm and secure. She knew she should move
hers, but for a moment, she allowed herself the comfort. "I
know you're a wonderful mother, a good friend, and caring
neighbor, sensitive to others' pain, open to God's plans for
your life—"

"Whoa, how do you know I'm open to God's plans for
my life?"

"You study your Bible, you go to church, you pray—if you didn't care what God had to say you wouldn't do all of that."

"Those other things. . .they sound good, but if I'm such a wonderful mother, how come my daughter has never been to a restaurant before? As you so aptly pointed out earlier, why doesn't she have playmates? Attend preschool?" Megan's words ended on a sob.

"Because her mother was hurt so badly by the world that she wants to protect her precious child from that? Is that so awful?" Holt almost whispered the words as he tightly held her hand.

Megan's head snapped up. "You know." She jerked her hand away and swiped at her tears with the back of it. "How long have you known?"

"From the beginning. She didn't tell me the whole story, but Annie Sampson jogged my memory."

Disbelief coursed through her. "Why didn't you run the other way as fast as you could?"

"And never have a chance to watch a sunset with you? Or see Sarah's delight at using a 'rooster' seat?" He smiled.

"Oh, Holt. You know what I mean. You shouldn't have come to the house the day we met. How much heartache you could have saved us if you hadn't."

&

Along with his usual prayer for patience, Holt sent a silent request for a large helping of wisdom. *Lord, give me the right words.*

"I can't speak for you, but there's not a heartache in this world that's big enough to make me give up one minute I've spent with you." He reached out and gently wiped away a tear with his thumb. He caressed her cheek for a few seconds then dropped a light kiss where his thumb had been. Leaning back in his chair, he realized it was time for her to speak her piece. "You want to tell me why I should have run?"

She allowed him to put his arm around her. In spite of the rocker arms between them, she leaned against him, as if absorbing his strength. "Barry swept me off my feet. Before I met him, I was strong and independent. 'Megan will really go places.' That's what people used to say. I was voted 'Most Likely to Succeed' in high school."

He grinned at this glimpse of her adolescent persona, but she didn't return his smile.

"I was voted 'Class Clown,'" Holt said.

"Were you really, or are you just saying that to make me smile?"

He grinned. "Both."

Her lips turned up for a second, then quickly changed back to an expression more appropriate for the dentist's chair.

"Anyway, after Barry and I became involved, nothing was as important as pleasing him. Sometimes I'd think maybe he wasn't being completely honest, but the dazzle in his smile would make me reconsider. We married not long after we started dating. I remember thinking how lucky I was that he chose me.

"He was a plant controller at Minton's in Jonesboro. So, not only did he make me go weak in the knees, he made a comfortable living. We were able to get a nice house right away. Barry wasn't satisfied with his job. He wanted to get into investments. He started small and had some small successes. One night, about a month after Sarah was born, he woke me at three in the morning and told me that he had a plan.

"He wanted to start a theme park in this area, where my mother's family was from. He wanted to use only local investors and bragged to me that he would turn the economy around. Make everyone in the area wealthy. I questioned the logic of this idea, and he pouted for a week, refusing even to speak to me. By the end of that time, I was miserable."

Holt squeezed her hand.

"After I'd reassured him of my support, his excitement bubbled over again. He made a list, and we went around to everyone we knew—my parents, my grandmother's friends, the people at church, local businessmen. He had a remarkable business plan. The park itself was sketched out on blueprint-type paper, and it looked impressive. Some people hated the idea. But plenty of others were very interested. Seeing their excitement convinced me that this could really work."

"Did you help him handle the investments?" Holt knew what had been insinuated in the papers, but from the moment he'd met Megan, he knew, as well as Annie Sampson did, that there was no way she'd be involved in anything dishonest. If it ever came up, he'd just have to be sure the voters knew it too.

"No. Barry had me go with him to make the initial contact with each person, but after that, I had nothing to do with the amounts invested or how the money was used."

Holt couldn't completely control his anger at a man who would use his wife as Barry Watson had. When Megan looked at their intertwined hands, he realized he was squeezing too tightly. "Oops." He offered a rueful half-grin as he relaxed his iron grip. "I guess I'm more than a little angry at what he did to you."

She shook her head. "I've run the gamut of emotions from fear to hurt to anger to forgiveness. There's no purpose in being mad at a dead man."

"No, I don't suppose there is. So did you find out before he died? Or after?"

"He began coming home later and looking worried, but whenever I'd ask him how things were going, he'd give me a flip answer and a thousand-watt smile.

"People started wanting concrete details on how the theme park was coming along. He'd kept the plans shrouded in secrecy as far as location and so on. One morning, I got up determined to make Barry tell me what was going on. By then I was beginning to see through the façade, and I wanted answers myself. After all, my mother had put her inheritance in this venture. I stomped into the exercise room ready for a confrontation and found Barry lying on the floor. An autopsy revealed he'd had a massive heart attack and died immediately."

"Megan, I can't imagine how hard that was for you."

This time it was she who squeezed his hand, then released it. She pushed her hair back from her face. "While we were planning the funeral, I realized that I would be the one to have to answer to all of those investors. I went through his papers looking for a clue. What I found was a catastrophe.

"When Barry realized he didn't have the investors to build on a grand scale, he'd reinvested their money without disclosing this fact to them. He'd lost it all. Now there was no money, no theme park, not even any land, and no Barry. All that was left to face the music was me." Tears welled up in her eyes again, and Holt devoutly wished he could have been there to stand by her during such a horrible time.

"Well, that's not really true. I had God to depend on. Thankfully, Barry had a life insurance policy that I had split up proportionally among all his investors, but it was nowhere near enough. One of the hardest things I've ever done was tell my own mother that because of me she'd lost all of that money Granny Lola had worked so hard for all her life. To this day I can't face her and my father." She shrugged. "In a way, in addition to everything else, Barry even took my parents from me." She tried to smile through her tears. "Well, that's all of my pity party. Heard enough? Aren't you glad you wore your running shoes tonight?"

"What I've heard is the story of a brave woman who let herself be taken in, then paid the price. You weren't dishonest, and when you discovered his deceit you were going to confront him." To Holt there was no question that she'd just ended up in a bad situation. So why was she still hiding?

"But don't you see?" She relaxed back against his arm. "It was too late." She raised her head and pushed to her feet. "Just like it's too late for us. Actually, there should have never been an 'us.' You have to have freedom, and I can't give you that. I'll never be free."

"Freedom is a state of mind, Megan."

"Fancy words can't make this go away. And if you won't run, I will."

"I'm not running." Holt stood and extended his hand to her.

Without saying a word, she turned and walked across the porch.

"Megan, you've got it all wrong."

She never turned around but just shook her head and slipped inside the house.

Long after her screen door slammed, Holt stood there looking at the little farmhouse. He would go home because it would be uncomfortable sleeping in his pickup, but he knew in his heart that he was far from giving up on Megan Watson.

ten

Holt didn't know what Megan would say when he showed up as if it were a regular Tuesday. He'd spent yesterday trying to convince himself just to let her go, but his heart wasn't so easily reclaimed.

He couldn't make her believe he wasn't worried about her past. How would he ever share his plans for the future? And if he was able to persuade her, could he be sure he was strong enough to stand by her, no matter what?

Lord, please help me to remember that Your opinion is the only one that matters.

Just as he pulled into the driveway, Megan and Sarah ran out of the house toward their van. The frantic look on Megan's face propelled him from his truck.

"It's Aunt Irene! She's fallen."

"Get in and I'll drive you. My truck's already running."

Without hesitation, Megan guided Sarah to Holt's truck and helped her into the backseat of the crew cab pickup, then she jumped in the front.

Holt glanced at Megan's pale face and reached over and took her hand. In spite of the summer heat, her fingers were ice cold. "Did she call 9-1-1?"

"Yes, just before she called me."

He jerked the vehicle into the elderly woman's long driveway.

"When we get up there," Megan said, in a low voice, "let Sarah stay outside and play with the puppies. I'll go in to be with Aunt Irene until the ambulance comes."

"Okay, but if you need me, promise you'll yell."

She nodded. Before the truck came to a complete stop, she jumped out and ran into the house. Holt noticed Aunt Irene's old green pickup had the tailgate down. Groceries were scattered on the ground and in the bed of the truck. Had the older woman fallen outside?

The puppies bounded toward Holt and Sarah as they walked across the yard. Holt hurriedly gathered the scattered groceries into the empty bags. When he'd finished he sank down on the porch, he hoped within earshot of the house, and watched the preschooler run and romp with the pups. He heard a couple of low moans from the living room and started to rise. Then he recognized Megan's voice, no longer frantic, but calm and soothing as she spoke to her elderly neighbor.

"How come we can't go inside?" Sarah stared at him, a frown marring her normally cheerful face. "Is Aunt Irene hurt bad?"

"I'm not sure." Holt didn't have much experience with children, but he remembered that even when he was young, he'd appreciated honesty. "She's hurting, but I think she's going to be okay."

"Don't you think she's gonna want me to hold her hand?" Her voice went up on the last word, and he could see a hint of tears in her eyes.

"Your mama's holding her hand. But there is something we can do."

"What?"

"Pray."

She nodded. "Will you do it?"

"Sure." Holt bowed his head.

"Wait!" Sarah yelled.

Holt looked up quickly. "What's wrong?"

She slipped her tiny hand into his. "We always hold hands when we pray."

He squeezed her hand and nodded, then bowed again. He waited for a second to see if she would think of something else. When she remained quiet, he began to speak. "Father, thank you so much for letting Sarah and me come to you in prayer today. We want to ask you to be with Aunt Irene. Please take away her pain and help her to get better quickly. In Jesus' name, amen."

He looked up to see Sarah's head still bowed. Her little voice broke the silence. "God? Thank you for Mr. Holt. Me and Mama like him a lot, 'cept he makes Mama cry sometimes. In Jesus' name, am—"

The squeal of sirens cut off the amen. Sarah jerked around with a start, then jumped into Holt's lap. He gathered her up and moved to the porch swing. It went against his grain not to be in the middle of the action, but he was here to help and right now Megan needed Sarah kept out of the way more than anything.

The EMTs hurried past them into the house. In what seemed no time at all, they rushed back past toting Aunt Irene on a stretcher. Holt looked at her ankle and cringed.

Megan was the last one to come out. She stepped onto the porch and watched as the paramedics loaded her friend into the ambulance. The forlorn look on her face propelled Holt to his feet, gently sliding Sarah to a standing position as well.

His legs seemed to move of their own volition as he walked across to the woman he'd come to care so much about. He folded her into his arms. She stiffened, then collapsed against him. He laid his cheek against the top of her head.

Sarah stood for a minute, as if frozen, then she burst forward and threw her arms around them together. They each released one arm to include the little girl in the embrace.

"We have to go to the hospital," Megan said. "Or at least I do."

"We'll all go." Taking into consideration Megan's stubbornness, Holt made sure his tone brooked no argument.

He led them to the truck and helped them in, then hurried around to climb in the driver's seat. As the truck bounced down the gravel road, Megan laid her head against the window.

"Aunt Irene's gonna be okay, Mama."

"I know it, Baby."

"She really is. Me and Mr. Holt prayed for her."

Megan turned and looked at Holt. "Thanks," she murmured. "That's great, Sarah."

For the rest of the trip to the hospital, Sarah rattled on to her imaginary friends about the importance of prayer. In spite of their worry, Holt and Megan exchanged a small smile.

"That's some girl you've got there." Holt was still a little stunned at Sarah's prayer.

"I like her."

"How is she?" He glanced at Megan. With something akin to the unspoken communication of a couple who'd been together for years, he realized she knew he hadn't wanted to say Aunt Irene's name where Sarah would hear.

"In pain. It's definitely broken. The bone was sticking out the skin."

"How did it happen? Could she tell you?"

Megan nodded. "She'd just gotten home from getting groceries. She climbed up into the truck and was straddling the tailgate. Somehow the latch gave away and the tailgate came down on her leg."

"How did she get into the house?"

"Apparently, she lay on the ground for awhile." Megan drew a shuddering breath but kept her voice low. "Then she dragged herself across the yard, up the steps, and into the house. She blacked out before she could reach the cordless phone. When she came to, she called 9-1-1, then me."

Holt could see the worry on her face. Odd how he'd always thought he could find the right thing to say in any situation. Since he'd met Megan, it seemed like his vocabulary had diminished. "I'm sorry."

She nodded but turned to stare out the window.

Suddenly, he remembered when he was on the debate team in high school. His mom had joked that if he ever met a girl who struck him speechless, he'd better hold on to her. Unfortunately, she hadn't told him what to do if the girl kept pushing him away.

❧

Even though he had plenty of both, some things are more important than good looks and charm, Megan thought, three days later, as she watched Holt help Aunt Irene into the car he'd borrowed. When he'd shown up today in the unfamiliar vehicle, he'd explained that he thought the car would be more comfortable for the elderly woman with her bulky walking cast.

Megan had already realized she was falling in love with Holt, but in the last few days, she'd realized something almost worse. She liked him. An incredible amount.

The tenderness in his eyes every time he looked at her was her undoing. He'd been so patient with Aunt Irene, and he'd been feeding the puppies twice a day while the elderly woman was in the hospital. Megan had told him she and Sarah could do it, but he'd insisted she had her hands full visiting the hospital.

She prayed that he wouldn't even look at her on the way home. Her resistance was weak, yet her reasons for not getting involved with him hadn't changed. If she really loved him, she'd do well to remember she could only bring him heartache in the end.

Aunt Irene rode in the front with Holt, so it looked like Megan's prayer was answered. But when they got the older woman settled in the den, with Sarah beside her showing off her favorite videos, Holt sought Megan out.

"What are you doing?"

She looked up. "I'm just putting away the groceries that didn't ruin."

"I carried them up to the porch when I fed the pups. If I'd had a key, I'd have put them away. Can I give you a hand?"

"No. I've got it under control." She busily arranged some canned goods on the shelf.

"You always have everything under control, don't you, Megan?" His voice was right at her ear. She stood stock-still. If she turned around their faces would be inches apart.

"No." She despised the tremble in her voice.

"Really?" he whispered. "What can't you control?"

"You."

"Turn around, Megan."

She pivoted slowly around and stared at him. His eyes were such a deep blue. They reminded her of the ocean, and just like the ocean, they had hidden depths. She could easily get lost in them.

"Megan."

"What?"

"I'm going to kiss you now. Is that okay?"

At his unexpected words, she raised her hand to her mouth to stifle a nervous giggle. It caught in her throat and emerged as a sort of silly sounding hiccup. She tried to shake her head, but instead she nodded slightly.

He lowered his mouth to hers, and she surrendered for a moment to the sweetness. Holt's kiss was like every good thing she'd ever seen, felt, or imagined all rolled into one.

Too soon, he raised his head to look at her. Emotion shone in his eyes. He cleared his throat. "Megan, I. . ." His voice was husky.

"Yes?" She felt as weightless as a feather on the wind.

"Please say you'll go with me to the picnic."

The words were so unexpected she chuckled, in spite of her befuddled senses. "Boy, you sure know how to take advantage of a girl's weak moment, don't you?"

He didn't say anything, but the dazed expression on his face made her sure that she wasn't the only one feeling a little funny.

"Please?"

She knew she had to say no. But the thought of spending more time with Holt before she had to break it off completely tempted her. She could imagine how many happy memories they could make over the holiday weekend. Memories that would have to sustain her for the rest of her life. "Okay."

Beaming, he dropped a light kiss on her cheek. "You won't be sorry."

She already was. She knew better than to lead a man on, but she'd allowed her heart to do the leading when her head should have taken the reins. "Listen, I'll go, but when we come back, that's it. It's over."

The happy expression on his face clouded, then quickly cleared. "I'll take what I can get for now, Meg. Who knows? Maybe I'll change your mind by then."

eleven

Holt glanced at Megan as they turned off the highway onto the gravel. "Nervous?"

"A little." She cast a glance to the back where Sarah was asleep, just as she had been most of the trip.

"They'll love you."

"Unless one of them remembers reading about me in the newspaper three years ago. Then they'll think I'm a gold-digger trying to get my hooks into you."

Holt laughed. "You don't know my family. If I like you, they'll like you." He paused, and the look he gave her brought the memory of their kiss rushing to the forefront of her mind. "And I definitely like you."

"Have they always been so accepting of your dates?"

"Are you fishing to see how many dates I've brought home?"

She grinned. "You wish."

"Yes, I do."

"Are you avoiding the question?"

"You'd make a good lawyer, you know that?"

She crossed her arms and regarded him intently. "I've only brought one woman to meet my folks, besides you."

"Is she the one who made you think about leaving the Batesville area?"

He sharply glanced at her, then back at the road. "You don't miss a thing, do you?" He ran his hand through his hair. "Yeah, that would be her. Her name is Gloria. Marshall Whitmore is her father."

"Did your family like her?"

"Oh, they tried, but no, not particularly."

"And this is supposed to be reassuring? I thought you said they'd like anyone you liked?"

"Well, Gloria was the exception."

"Want to tell me what happened?"

❧

Holt nodded. Megan had a right to know what an idiot he'd been, and if someone at the get-together today mentioned it. . . He took a deep breath and told her about the last weekend he'd spent in the Whitmore's colonial home. It had been a little over a year ago. He'd awakened early and slipped downstairs to get a cup of coffee. He didn't realize Gloria and her father were already in the kitchen until he'd heard their voices.

"It won't be too much longer, Dear, and you'll be having your morning coffee in the governor's mansion."

"It seems like forever. Holt still has to finish out this term as senator. Then we have to convince him to run for governor."

"It won't take much convincing. That's one reason I picked him. I have a feeling he's had his eye on the governor's chair for a good while now."

Holt stood at the doorway. His conscience tried to push him on inside. But his feet remained fixed to the floor.

"He wouldn't have had a chance without you around to smooth his edges, Daddy," Gloria purred. "Arkansas may be a little backwards, but they would never elect a hillbilly cowboy to be the governor."

"Careful, Dear, that hillbilly is going to be your ticket to the moon and mine too, if you play your cards right. You're going to have to try harder to appreciate him."

Gloria's tinkling laugh rang through the hallway.

"Appreciate him? All I have to do is make sure he keeps on appreciating me. He's going to ask me to marry him tonight. I just know it."

A slight sniff pulled him back to the present. Startled, Holt glanced over at Megan. Her eyes were brimming with tears. "Oh, Meg, I didn't mean to make you cry. Even though I didn't know it then, my heart wasn't really involved anyway, just my pride."

"What did you do?"

"Well, I was afraid I'd say things I'd regret if I confronted them right then, so I just slipped back upstairs, packed my bags, and left."

He grimaced. "The most irritating thing was Gloria was right. I had been about to propose."

"So what did they say when you did confront them?" Megan asked.

Holt shook his head. "I never did. It just seemed safer politically to leave it."

"That doesn't sound like the Holt McFadden I know."

"Are you saying I strike you as confrontational?" He hoped his joke would change the subject. Even though he was driving, he felt her gaze, unwavering, on his face.

"No, that's not what I'm saying. It just seems to me that when wrong is done you have to confront it, in a Christian way, of course, and let God deal with the consequences."

Holt squirmed in his seat and looked out the window at the rolling hills and cattle. She obviously wasn't in politics, or she'd know the wrong confrontation could be political suicide. "It's beautiful here, isn't it?"

❧

Megan considered trying to make Holt see the truth in what she was saying, but she thought of her own situation and decided she'd better save the sermons for herself. "Yes, it is. Too bad Aunt Irene didn't come. She likes seeing new places."

"Unlike her hermit neighbor, huh?" Holt teased, visibly grateful the conversation was back on a lighter level. "I was surprised you agreed to come at all, but especially after she said she'd rather pass on this trip because of her ankle."

Megan gave him a rueful grin. "I was going to back out, but she said her sister was coming in to stay with her this weekend, and that I'd just be in the way hovering over her."

"Good old Aunt Irene. I can always count on her to help me out."

"Does your brother own this land?"

"Yep. On both sides of the road. It belonged to my grandparents, but they retired to Florida. At first, Cade leased it for a boys' ranch, but when he and Annalisa decided to get married and adopt the boys, he bought it."

"How many boys?"

"Three, plus Annalisa's little sister, Amy, will probably be there."

She noticed he knew without question that she was wondering about the crowd. "How many people all together?"

"Let's see. . .Six in Cade's family, counting Amy, then Mom and Dad and Aunt Gertie make nine. My brother, Clint—he's the fireman—and my little brother, Jake."

"Little brother?"

Holt smiled. "Jake's a grown man, but sometimes that's hard for me to realize."

"Are Clint and Jake either one married?" She was listening to Holt's rundown on his family, but she was mentally calculating the number of people.

"Nope. Clint's too busy putting out fires, and Jake has a

girlfriend he's somewhat serious about. Oh, she might be there today."

"So there should be around twelve, not counting us," she said.

"That's a fair estimate, but at a McFadden holiday there are always at least one or two lonely souls thrown in for good measure. My mama can't stand for anyone to be alone on a holiday. Not even the Fourth of July."

"Fourteen then, plus us."

He nodded. "Yeah, or twenty. I said 'at least' one or two. Has been up to ten or fifteen."

She pressed her hand to her stomach. "I don't think I can do this, Holt."

"You don't have a choice, beautiful Meg." He grinned and whipped the truck into a driveway. "We're here."

❧

Holt had enjoyed teasing Megan too much to tell her, but he'd made sure they were the first guests to arrive. He'd figured the fewer people she had to get used to at a time, the better.

They stepped up on the front porch and allowed a drowsy Sarah the privilege of ringing the doorbell. As they waited for someone to answer, Holt put his arm around Megan's waist. "You're trembling," he whispered.

"Tell me something I don't know."

"Okay." He leaned in closer to her ear, and the faint scent of her shampoo had him trembling himself. "I'm falling in love with you."

She jerked her head up to stare at him, and her eyes widened, just as the front door opened.

"Holt!" Cade shook his hand enthusiastically, then pulled him into a bear hug. When he released Holt, he smiled. "And you must be Megan."

She nodded, but Holt noticed she looked dazed. His timing could have definitely been better, but he felt as if he'd held the words in as long as he could.

❧

Unmindful of her turmoil, Cade continued with the introductions, and Megan did her best to concentrate on what he was saying. He squatted down in front of Sarah. "And you're Sarah, aren't you? I thought Holt was pulling my leg when he told me he was bringing a beautiful princess with him. But I see now he really did."

Sarah's whole face lit up with her smile. "Are there kids here?"

"Sure are. Come on in." Cade stood and led them into the living room where a young girl of nine or ten was lying on the floor, drawing.

She looked up and waved.

"This is Annalisa's sister and my favorite sister-in-law, Amy." He winked at the child, and she returned his wink with an exaggerated one of her own. Megan could see that Holt wasn't the only McFadden brother who was good with kids. "Amy, this is my brother Holt and his friends, Megan and Sarah."

Sarah hurried over to Amy and plopped down beside her. "Can I color?"

"Sure."

Megan was pleased to notice that Sarah had no trouble meeting strangers, in spite of the sheltered life she'd led. Now if only Sarah's mother could adapt as well. It had just been too long since she'd attended a social gathering.

Cade led them into the kitchen. A tall, striking brunette was putting the finishing touches on a flag cake. The woman hugged Holt, then Cade pulled her close to him. "Megan, this is my wife, Annalisa." Pride emanated from his voice.

As the women offered each a "nice to meet you," Cade nodded toward the kitchen door. "Holt, you want to come with me to check on the barbecue?"

Holt glanced at Megan, and she nodded. In spite of her assent, her heart pounded in her chest as he followed his older brother out the door, leaving her alone with a stranger.

*

"So how serious is it?"

"You cut straight to the chase, don't you, Cade?"

"Always."

"I'm in love with her, but she thinks her past will ruin my career."

"Will it?"

Holt shrugged. "It could, I guess. But isn't love supposed to be more important than politics?"

"It's supposed to be," Cade replied thoughtfully. "Just be sure you can deal with the consequences."

Holt couldn't keep the sharpness from his tone. "What wouldn't you give up for Annalisa?"

"This is not about me. I just know how important your career is to you." Cade's answer was gentle as he lifted the cover of the massive barrel grill. "I can tell by how defensive you are that the idea scares you. You've worked hard to get where you are, and even though I had my doubts at first, it does seem that God wants you there. There's no shame in not wanting to endanger that."

Holt forced himself to calm down. It had taken a long time for him to convince his brother that his political career was God's will. He couldn't blame Cade for being honest, and he deserved honesty in return. "My fear is that I'll let Megan down if she needs me. I've been asking God to give me the courage to stand firm. But, really, the answer is no, I don't believe her past will ruin my career, regardless of what she thinks. She was proven innocent of any wrongdoing. Besides that's old news. It was three years ago. People have forgotten by now."

"You always overestimate the good in people, Holt." Cade clapped a hand on his shoulder. "The eternal optimist. But I wouldn't have you any other way."

"I had to be an optimist to balance you out. You've always expected the worst."

Cade glanced over to the porch where Annalisa and Megan were now standing in earnest conversation. "Not anymore."

Holt laughed. "I know what you mean. Amazing how they can turn us inside out, isn't it?"

"And make us welcome the upheaval." Cade joined his brother's laughter.

❧

"Sounds like the two oldest McFadden brothers are glad to see each other," Annalisa commented as the masculine laughter floated across the yard.

"I know Holt was excited about coming." In spite of her phobia of meeting new people, Megan found herself drawn to this woman who towered over her in height and had a smile as bright as the sunshine.

"Cade couldn't wait for y'all to get here. He kept hearing something and running to the front window to check. Like a little kid at Christmas." Annalisa smiled at Megan. "More than anything, I think he wanted to meet the woman who'd turned his little brother's world upside-down."

"Me?" Megan squeaked. She hadn't expected this. She was braced for a morning of recipe and weather discussions, but apparently, Holt's sister-in-law didn't believe in surface conversation.

"Yes, you."

"Actually, we're not serious." Megan forced herself to say the words, because she couldn't bear for her new friend to hate her when she found out Megan and Holt were no longer seeing each other after this was over.

"Uh-huh. You sound like me before Cade and I worked things out."

"What do you mean?"

"You're in denial. You look at Holt like you're dying of thirst and he's a giant glass of ice water. He looks at you the same way. So, what's the problem?"

From anyone else, the question would have seemed rude, but Annalisa's concern was so obviously genuine, Megan wasn't offended.

"More than you can imagine. I'm not good for him, Annalisa. Let's just leave it at that. If you love your brother-in-law, the last thing you'll want to do is encourage his relationship with me."

"You have a secret."

"What?" Megan didn't know what to say. The woman was uncanny.

"All the signs are there. Something in your past makes you think he'd be better off without you." She gave Megan an appraising look. "Let's see, he's determined to go forward with this political career of his, and you're obviously crazy about him. . . ," Megan felt the heat rise in her cheeks at this observation. "So you must think you'd be a detriment to it."

"Did anyone ever tell you that you're a little bit. . ." In spite of Annalisa's frank assessment of her situation, Megan didn't want to hurt her feelings.

"Pushy? Nosy?" Annalisa laughed and twisted her dark brown hair up on top of her head with one hand. "I've been told that a time or two. I'm not really this bad usually, but I don't know. . .it just felt like you and I clicked as soon as we started talking in the kitchen. When I looked at you, I could see so much of myself when I first came to the Circle M." Her smile faded a bit and her brown eyes looked slightly troubled. "You're not really offended, are you?"

Megan laughed. "I should be, but I'm not." She looked again at the tall, confident woman and couldn't imagine what about her would remind Annalisa of herself. "Do you really want to hear about my past?"

"Sure." She looked out to where the men were striding toward the barn. "It looks like they'll be busy for awhile. You can tell me while we make a salad."

They walked back into the kitchen. Megan waited until she was armed with a knife and a cutting board, then began to talk as she chopped fresh vegetables.

After Megan had spilled the whole sorry tale of Barry's betrayal, Ivo's persecution, the authorities questioning her, and her and Sarah moving to the farm, Annalisa shook her head. "That's a lot for one woman to bear alone."

Megan appreciated the sympathy. For years, she'd kept it all hidden inside. Letting it out felt like a cool shower. "I really wasn't alone. God has stood by me all along. I've never doubted Him. People are harder to trust."

"You're my kind of gal, Meg." Annalisa banged a head of lettuce on the counter and tossed the core in the industrial-size garbage can. "But life's so much better when you learn to trust again." She deftly broke up a large salad. "Just to prove it, I'm going to trust you with a secret." She laughed. "That sounded noble, didn't it? Truth is, I'm dying to tell someone. Cade's going to announce it today, but. . ." She slapped her forehead gently with her hand. "I'm doing it again. Cade says I always try to tell the end of the story, before the beginning."

Megan couldn't keep from laughing. "Whoa, breathe, Girl. Tell me your secret before you hyperventilate."

In spite of the fact that they were in the kitchen with the swinging doors closed, Annalisa leaned toward Megan and lowered her voice to an excited whisper. "I'm pregnant!"

"Oh, Annalisa! That's wonderful. When are you due?"

The two women spent the next half hour sharing confidences. When everything was ready for the coming crowd, Megan thought back on what the brunette had shared about her and Cade's troubles getting together. They'd had such a hard time working things out. Could there be hope for her and Holt?

"It's almost time for the others to get here. Shall we go rest our weary bones until they come?"

Annalisa's question brought her back to the present. "Sure." Megan realized with amazement that forging a friendship with Annalisa had almost completely erased her nervousness about meeting the crowd. If everyone was as nice as her hostess was, this day should actually be fun.

twelve

Clint was the first to arrive. Holt and Cade both wrapped him in a bear hug. Megan was surprised by this show of affection. Her own brothers were good friends, but she didn't remember ever seeing them hug.

Although he was a little serious for her taste, Megan immediately liked him. He fit the image of a fireman—strong and able to protect one against anything.

Three boys bounded into the room. "Uncle Clint!" The youngest one leaped onto Clint's lap, and the other two hugged him.

Cade performed the introductions, proudly introducing his three newly adopted sons to Megan and Sarah.

The doorbell rang as soon as he finished, and the rest of the afternoon was a blur of people coming and going. Mostly coming. Holt sought Megan out numerous times, smiling each time when she assured him she was fine and encouraged him to go catch up with his relatives. She noticed that Annalisa never strayed far from her side, though, and, in spite of her newfound confidence, she was grateful.

She'd always thought one could learn a lot about a person by getting to know their family. In Holt's case, this seemed to be true, because everywhere she looked, she saw humor, character, and love.

❧

Jake and Cade were sipping lemonade when Holt joined them by the fence. The horses that were in the pasture had hurried over to get their share of the attention, and all three of the McFadden brothers were happy to oblige. Their love of horses was one thing they all shared.

"Hey, Jake!" Holt clapped his youngest brother on the back. "Good to see you." He looked around. "Did you bring Tami?"

The bright grin on Jake's face faded slightly. "No, she couldn't come today. She had to do a photo shoot."

Holt nodded, but he knew his brother was let down. Jake had been excited when his girlfriend had first made a break into modeling, but lately he seemed to be worried that the glamorous life was pulling her away from him. Holt couldn't deny he had the same concerns, but he said nothing.

"Clint loves horses more than any of us. Where is he?" Jake asked, in an obvious attempt to change the subject.

Cade shook his head. "There's no telling."

"Apparently their unit responded to a house fire yesterday afternoon, and they didn't get the dad out."

Holt shook his head. He couldn't imagine.

"I'll go talk to him," Holt said.

The other two nodded. All of the brothers were close, but Holt and Clint were only eleven months apart and related to each other almost like twins.

☙

Before beginning his search, Holt checked in on Megan and Sarah. Megan had found a champion in Cade's wife. The two of them were taking turns swapping stories about kids with Holt's mom and aunt, and all of them appeared to be having a ball. In spite of their age differences, four-year-old Sarah and ten-year-old Amy were united against the three boys who teased them unmercifully. Everyone in the house really seemed to be enjoying themselves, but Clint was nowhere to be found.

Following his instinct, Holt hurried out to the barn. Sure enough, Clint had sought comfort from the horses, a habit Holt remembered well from their childhood.

"Hey."

Clint swung around to face him. "Hey." His attempt at a smile was poor, to say the least. The deep creases etched on his forehead seemed to have sprung up overnight.

"Cade said you had a bad time yesterday."

"Yeah."

"Want to talk about it?"

"Nope, but thanks for asking."

Holt smiled at his brother who was so careful with others feelings even though he was hurting. "Clint, I'm really sorry, man."

"I know. There's nothing anyone can do."

"Yeah, I know."

"I should have gotten to him."

"How do you figure?"

"I just should have. If I'd turned the other way. . ."

Holt shuddered at how close he might have come to losing his brother. If he overreacted, though, he knew Clint would clam up. " 'If' is the biggest word in the English language. If you'd turned the other way, you might have been trapped along with him. The possibilities are endless, Clint. Please don't blame yourself."

"Thanks, Bro."

"I'm sorry."

"Yeah, me too. I guess it goes with the job." Clint looked up at him with a sad half-smile. He gave the horse a final pat on the nose. "Let's go back up to the house before Mama gets worried about her boys."

"Yeah, because she won't let you off the hook as easy as I did if she gets wind of trouble."

"You've got that right." Clint's grin was still tinged with grief but closer to the real thing this time. "Has she grilled you about Megan yet?"

"No, but she seems to like her a lot."

"Why wouldn't she? I think you've got a keeper there, Holt."

"Yeah, me too. I'm hoping today will help me convince her of that."

"Uh-oh, if you're counting on your family to sway her, maybe you should have told Mom to leave Uncle Harold and Aunt Lou at home."

"Actually, I'm pretty sure Megan has a few family difficulties of her own. Maybe it will help for her to see that my family isn't perfect."

Clint smiled. "Only you could see the bright side of their constant bickering."

❧

Holt glanced over at Megan who was trying valiantly to keep her head from bumping the ceiling. He eased off the accelerator even more. "Cade needs to get this road fixed," he grumbled.

"I–I–I l–l–like it," Sarah said, her voice vibrating with the motion as she bounced in the backseat. She giggled.

Megan offered Holt a huge grin. "She 'l–l–likes' it, Holt. Don't be a spoilsport." She glanced back at the other trucks, loaded with people, following them down the grassy path. "Besides, calling this a 'road' strikes me as a stretch, even for a politician."

Holt laughed. "I guess you're right. But it's the fastest way to the river. And at least it's not a long trip." He pulled in beside Cade's SUV and parked. Jake's truck and Clint's fire engine red Jeep were already there. A small grove of trees blocked a view of the river from the field.

Megan waved at Annalisa who still sat in their vehicle. Holt waited patiently, as well, until all the other trucks were parked. When the last engine was dead, everyone jumped out, grabbed their blankets and lawn chairs, and headed toward an opening in the trees.

Holt smiled as Megan helped his Aunt Gertie down the steep sloping trail that led to the river's sandy bank. Sarah carried the elderly lady's water bottle. Holt's mother had her arm at Sarah's shoulder, making sure the little girl didn't fall.

When they got to the bottom, Holt's mother and father and aunt and uncle, as well as Aunt Gertie, set their chairs in a loose circle around the small campfire that Jake and Clint had come a few minutes early to build. Holt and Cade spread out blankets for all the others.

Juan, Tim, and Matthew hurried to the river and began to engage in a rock-skipping contest. Amy stood up from where she helped Annalisa smooth out their blanket and ran over to Sarah. "Want to go skip rocks?"

Sarah cast an uncertain look at her mother. Megan nodded and the preschooler jumped up and followed Amy to join the competition. When Amy skipped a flat stone ten times, even the boys whooped congratulations, and from then on, the girls were accepted. Holt watched as Tim, the youngest, carefully showed Sarah how to hold a rock.

"She sure is concentrating, isn't she?" Holt said quietly.

Megan smiled. "Yes, I told you she never gives up either, so we may still be here this time tomorrow."

Holt leaned over and whispered in her ear. "I can think of worse places to be than sitting next to you on a blanket for twenty-four hours." He teasingly nuzzled her hair.

Megan slapped at the air. "Holt!" she hissed. "Your mom and dad are right there. What will they think?"

"That I'm an incredibly blessed man?" He couldn't contain a grin.

"Oh, fine. If you're going to act like that, then I'm wasting my time trying to reason with you." Holt noticed her smile belied her irritated words.

"C'mon, kiddos, it's time to start," Cade called to the boys and girls skipping rocks. When the children were all seated, Holt noticed a flash of discomfort flit across Megan's face. She'd asked him what to expect, and he'd done his best to explain this family celebration, but she still seemed nervous.

❧

Megan squirmed a little on the blanket as Holt's dad, Jeb, stood and looked around at his family and friends. When she was young, she'd gone to camp and they'd had campfire "devotionals." She'd asked Holt if that was what they were doing down here by the river, but his answer had been cryptic. "Sort of. You'll just have to wait and see."

"Today we celebrate our independence." Jeb's voice carried to all the people present in spite of the ripple of the water in the background. "Our independence and our freedom as a country." He glanced around the circle. "But freedom isn't only about being an American. Freedom is about being part of your family and, most importantly, being a part of God's family."

"Let's pray." Jeb bowed his head and all the others did the same. "Father, thank you so much for this wonderful country you have blessed us with. We know there are many problems in America, but we are so thankful to have the freedom to try to change things that are wrong and, most of all, to have the freedom to worship You. Bless each one present here tonight, Lord. In our freedom, God, please bind us together, and let us lean on each other in our times of need. Thank You for your Son, who died to give us the most precious freedom of all. In His name, amen."

Megan felt the tears edging the corners of her eyes. Annalisa pulled out a small packet of tissues from her pocket. She took one for herself, leaned over, and handed one to Megan. "Holidays with this family. . ." she whispered, with a shrug. "I've learned to come prepared."

Megan mouthed thank you, just as Jake started a song asking God to "Bind us together." The others quickly joined in and, as the sunset painted beautiful swirls of color across the sky above their heads, their voices united in a sweet song that resounded through the river valley.

When the song ended, Jeb looked out over the group. "Who else wants to say something?"

No one moved for a minute, then Cade hopped to his feet. "I do."

Cade looked at his wife. "Most of you know that Annalisa and I were both imprisoned by our pasts when we met. Though a little over a year ago, I was a bachelor, with no visible ties, as I look at my precious family. . . ," his gaze lingered on each of the three boys and Amy, then came back to Annalisa's face, ". . .I thank God that by Him bringing us all together we have finally been freed."

He looked around the campfire. "Who's next?"

Megan's heart jumped in her chest. Would they expect her to speak? She admired Jeb's obvious strength in God and Cade's devotion to his family, but there was no way she could talk, especially about being free. Megan would never be truly free of her past.

"Don't worry. It's volunteer only." Holt's reassuring voice sounded right next to her ear.

She nodded, relieved, and brought her attention back to the campfire. Fourteen-year-old Juan had stood and was looking at his feet.

He kicked the sand softly and cleared his throat. "Um. . . when I was running with the gang on the street, I thought I was free. Free to make my own decisions. Free to have fun. Free to get in trouble. Then I came here. Now I know that what I thought was freedom then was a lie. The love of my family and my God. . .I wish I could tell my friends how much they're missing." He swiped a tear from his cheek and sat down, ducking his head as Cade clapped his hand on his shoulder.

Megan felt the tears finally overflow and spill down her cheeks. Annalisa reached over and squeezed her hand, then released it.

Holt's mother stood and smiled at each person in the circle, love apparent on her face, even in the firelight. "I'm thankful for the freedom of being a mom. A mother can say things that other people can't. So when someone in my family has a problem. . . ," she looked pointedly at Clint, ". . .I have the freedom to find out what's wrong. I'm not being nosy. It's just my job." Everyone chuckled. "Anybody else have something to say?" When no one responded, she raised an eyebrow at Holt. "Senator? Can you get me out of this with some words of wisdom on freedom?"

"Sure, Mom." Holt stood, and his mother sank back into her chair.

Megan tensed. Surely he wouldn't say anything personal. It was going to be hard enough never seeing his family again, much less leaving them with the wrong impression. She breathed a sigh of relief when his words were purely patriotic.

"I don't know about words of wisdom, but most of you know I have definite thoughts on freedom." Megan watched in fascination as they all nodded. "In spite of its name. . . ," He grinned, ". . .freedom is not free. It's very costly. Many have died so that we can enjoy the liberties we too often take for granted.

"As Dad mentioned earlier, we're so blessed to live in a country where we can worship God without worrying that we'll be persecuted by the government for doing so. So the next time you go into a church building and you don't have to look over your shoulder to see if anyone is watching, remember your fellow countrymen who died to give you that right."

He stood in silence for a minute then he nodded at Megan "I know I promised no campaign speeches, but this doesn't really qualify, because I'm pretty sure everyone here was going to vote for me anyway."

"I wouldn't be overconfident, if I were you," Jake called Megan joined in the outburst of laughter.

"Okay, well, maybe not." Holt pasted a mock look of uncertainty on his face and sank back down on the blanket.

After the laughter had completely died down, Cade stood and started a song. The rest of the group rose and joined in. The song of thankfulness wafted up to the night sky and given the sincerity ringing out in each voice, Megan had no trouble imagining the words reaching all the way to heaven.

thirteen

"You have no idea how tough it is to set up a fireworks extravaganza while you're being closely watched by an over-anxious fireman." Jake grinned at the group who had all moved up to the open field, a large portion of which was freshly plowed for the occasion.

"Yeah, if Jake had his way, you'd each get those little buzzer fireworks under your chairs," Clint called from a good distance away where he was busily setting up bottle-rockets.

Everyone laughed, and Jake held up his hand. "Now wait a minute. We could have done it like you wanted, I guess, and just pass out those little snap and pop thingies. But it just doesn't seem like much of a show without ever lighting a match. We couldn't really call it "fire" works then, could we?"

Holt laughed as his brothers kept up their impromptu comedy routine while they worked. Even though Clint's heart obviously wasn't in it, Holt was glad he was here instead of all alone in his apartment in Little Rock.

Holt had an easy arm around Megan's shoulder, and her laughter did his heart a world of good. She'd really opened up since she'd been here. She and Sarah both blended in with his family seamlessly.

She's everything I've ever prayed for in a wife. Now if I could just convince her.

When it became obvious that the show was about to start, Cade and Annalisa stretched out on their blanket, and the four children piled around them. Holt and Megan exchanged a smile when Sarah scooted over next to Amy.

Holt leaned back with his hands behind his head and soon Megan did the same. With her there beside him, looking up at the starlit sky, he felt so close to her. She turned her head toward him just as he looked at her. Their noses were almost touching.

"Thank you for including me." Her voice was for his ears only.

"You're—" A beautiful fountain of gold exploded above them, cutting off his reply.

Holt watched in fascination as the gold reflection played on Megan's face. Her bow-shaped mouth formed a soundless O of surprise and delight.

When the second explosion came, she looked back to him. "You're supposed to be watching the fireworks, not me."

Holt shrugged. "Don't forget. It's a free country."

Her giggle was muffled by the rat-tat-tat of firecrackers.

❧

"Will you brush mine?"

Megan glanced in the mirror at Sarah and nodded. It was late, but Megan had been incredibly keyed up by the emotional night. When she sat down to brush her hair, she thought Sarah was already asleep in the guest bed they were to share.

She pulled her daughter up on the vanity bench beside her and began to brush her hair.

"I like Mr. Holt, don't you?"

"Yes, Sweetie, I do." Megan wanted to say so much more. . .to tell her not to hope for too much, to warn her of giving her heart, but none of it was appropriate conversation with a four year old.

"Everybody else is nice too, aren't they?"

"Um-hum." Megan brushed Sarah's long hair, and the rhythm was about to put her to sleep.

"I like Amy. . ." Sarah stifled a yawn with her hand.

Megan nodded.

"She teached me to skip a rock. Don't tell Lucy, but I think that makes Amy my very best friend. Don't you?" This time she didn't bother to raise her hand to cover the yawn.

The question faded to silence, and within a minute, her small body molded against Megan's side. A peek in the mirror revealed long eyelashes feathered across her rosy cheeks.

Megan carefully lifted her daughter and placed her in the bed, then hurried to finish with her own bedtime rituals. After she turned off the light, she remembered thinking earlier that she would never be free as long as she lived. But when she looked at Annalisa and all she'd overcome, she found her heart yearning for her own Independence Day. Could God make that happen?

Her prayers were jumbled but earnest, as she lay in the dark, alternately asking God for freedom from her past and begging Him to help her be strong enough to let Holt go.

❧

The next afternoon, Megan turned to take one more look at the Circle M. She'd enjoyed every minute of her time there with Holt's family. She was so thankful he'd talked her into coming.

"Was it as bad as you thought it would be?"

"I didn't think—"

"Oh, come on now, don't say that. You thought it would be horrible. I could see it in your face." Holt pulled the crew cab pickup onto the gravel road.

"I liked everybody!" Sarah piped up from the backseat.

"Especially Jake. He's nice. He caught a frog for me. And he helped me put it down Tim's back." The last words were smothered by a yawn.

"Was there another Jake there besides my baby brother?" Holt asked Megan in a whisper.

She laughed. "Not that I know of."

"That comment I made earlier about him being a grown man? I might have been a little premature in that announcement." He shrugged and maneuvered the truck down the bumpy road.

"I thought he was nice too. I felt sorry for him that his girlfriend didn't end up coming. I know he was disappointed, but it was really cool that he didn't mind playing with the kids."

"Yeah, he's always a good sport."

"I loved your parents. They remind me of my own."

"Really?" Holt's shock was evident in his voice, in spite of his obvious attempt to cover it.

"Yes, really." Megan looked out the windows. "Holt, you should know. . .the problems I have with my parents. I may not have made it clear before. They're my problems, not theirs."

"I find that hard to believe."

Megan was surprised how much Holt's unconditional support of her meant. "My parents never acted like it was my fault that they lost their money in Barry's investments, but I knew it was."

Holt nodded. "I see." He glanced at her, and she was surprised to realize he really did see. "Your pride just won't let you turn to them?"

"That's it." Megan glanced at her hands. "That doesn't make me much of a daughter, does it?"

"I imagine your parents would beg to differ."

"Who knows? I guess I haven't really given them a chance. Deep down they're probably glad. There's a lot less shame to deal with when I'm not around." Though the words stuck in her throat, she forced them out. "You should probably remember that."

"I think you—"

"Cade and Annalisa are absolutely wonderful, aren't they?"

He raised an eyebrow at her interruption, and she stared at him, pleading with her eyes for him not to pursue the subject.

"Yes, they are." He spoke softly. "They give me hope. Don't they you?"

"Your Aunt Gertie was really fun too. I can see why you love her so much."

Holt gave her a wry grin at her management of the conversation and nodded.

"And Clint. . ." Megan remembered how she'd felt almost a physical kick to the stomach by the pain she'd seen in Clint's eyes. "He's really a gentle giant, isn't he? He was obviously upset about something, but he still worried about whether his mama needed another glass of lemonade."

Holt filled her in briefly on the cause of Clint's distress.

"It must be a difficult job—holding someone else's life in your hands." Megan looked over at Holt and was struck by a foreign thought. "As much as I give you a hard time about politics, you hold people's lives in your hands too."

"Whoa." Holt pretended to pull back on the steering wheel. "Was that really an almost-positive thing you just said about politicians?"

She laughed. "Maybe. But don't get used to it."

"Don't worry. I won't figure on getting one of those comments from you more than once a year."

In spite of the heat, a shiver ran up her spine. She distinctly remembered telling him that when they got home from the family reunion, their relationship was over. But he talked as if a future together was a foregone conclusion. "Once a year, huh?"

He cast a sideways glance at her as he pulled off the gravel onto the highway. "You mean I might get compliments from you more often?"

She glanced at the backseat. Sarah had already fallen fast asleep. She'd played hard at the Circle M. "You know what I said before we came. . ." She swallowed against the telltale lump in her throat. "Holt, nothing has really changed."

Without warning, Holt whipped the truck into an empty church parking lot. When they stopped moving, he turned to her. "Megan, everything has changed." He reached up to reposition his cowboy hat, a habit she found endearing. He grinned sheepishly when he realized he didn't have it on, then ran his fingers through his hair instead. "Did you hear what I said to you on Cade's porch yesterday morning before he opened the door?"

"Yes." She spoke softly so as not to wake Sarah, but her voice trembled.

"Don't you feel anything for me?"

"Oh, Holt. You know I do. But if you and I. . . If I allow you. . . Being with me is suicide for your career." The tears that had been hovering fell onto her cheeks in big hot drops. "We can't do it."

"Don't you trust God?"

"You know I do."

"Don't you think He can handle my career?"

She knew where this was going, but she had to nod.

"Then why don't we let Him do His job?"

Silence filled the cab, broken only by the gentle snoring of Sarah from the backseat. Megan's mind whirled. Could she do it? Could she give Holt's career and her past over to God?

"Please, Megan."

Her jumbled bedtime prayers came to her mind. She had to try. "Okay, Holt. I'll give it my best shot."

He put his arm around her shoulders and pulled her close. She looked up into his dark eyes and thought she would drown. He leaned down, and she held her breath.

"Why are we stopped?"

Megan jumped with a nervous giggle and looked in the backseat. Sarah's eyes weren't open, but she'd awakened just enough to realize the vehicle had quit moving. Megan frantically motioned for Holt to start the truck and pull back on the road.

He started the motor but paused with his hand on the gearshift. "A promise is a promise whether it's sealed with a kiss or not, right?" he asked softly.

"Definitely," she whispered.

Apparently satisfied, he eased back onto the highway and headed home.

fourteen

Holt carried his cup of coffee outside. Standing on his porch, he breathed in the fresh air and thanked God for blessing him in so many ways. The moments just before sunrise were his favorite time of day. The sky was like an untouched canvas just waiting to see what wondrous images God would paint.

Today was even more special than most. Megan had agreed to go beyond friendship. His feet barely touched the ground as he walked out to the end of the driveway to get the newspapers.

Around here, a person got two for the price of one. There was the well-respected statewide paper, then there was what Holt considered the advertising one. It was disguised as a newspaper, with a few news stories, but was mainly a vehicle for advertising. Holt had a daily subscription to the statewide paper, but the other one came once a week and today was the lucky day.

Careful not to spill his coffee, he bent down and scooped them both up and walked back to sit in his glider chair on the porch. He scanned the headlines of the one he paid for, then finding nothing of great interest, flipped open the other one.

Of their own volition, his arms flew out—one knocking the coffee to the wooden floor where the cup shattered – and the other one dropping the offending paper on the floor beside the broken pieces. His heart pounded against his ribcage. How had this happened?

He laid his head against the back of the chair and prayed as he never had before. He hoped the Lord could make sense of the pleading of his soul, because he knew his anger was making his words irrational. After a few minutes, still shaking with fury but able to at least think, he picked up the paper again. A skillfully taken picture of him and Megan was above the lead story.

The photo had to have been taken when they were leaving The Fish House. Holt had put his arm protectively at her back, and she'd turned to say thank you. But in the picture, her eyes had taken on a seductive slant and his arm appeared to be draped in more of an amorous embrace than one of protection. Aunt Irene and Sarah had been flanking them, but in the picture, there was no evidence of others. The headline read "SENATOR HOLT McFADDEN—CHAMPION OF THE ELDERLY?"

The article stopped barely short of libel as it recanted Megan's past. After mentioning Holt's very public stance of being on the side of the elderly, the reporter said an "unnamed source" close to the couple had confirmed they were definitely "an item." The words "conflict of interest" and "ulterior motive" were tossed around like the bad clichés they were. The piece ended with an assurance that this reporter would make sure the public was informed if it looked like Megan planned to start seeking investments for any new venture and was aided by the senator.

Holt went hot, then cold, then hot again. He was shaking with a fury deeper than any he'd ever known.

Oh, Lord, give me Your heart. Allow me to see this reporter with your eyes.

Love your enemies and pray for those who persecute you. The familiar verses resounded in Holt's head.

*Father, please be with the writer of this article and help him to see
the pain his untrue words have caused. Give him a contrite heart.*

Each word, though not spoken aloud, still seemed to be
forced through gritted teeth. Holt wanted to pray such different things for the man who had ruined his chances of having the woman he loved.

He had to get to her. Maybe he could keep her from getting her paper. Maybe he could convince her to go away with
him until it all died down and she'd never even have to know
it had been printed. Maybe. . .

He stepped inside the front door and kicked off his slip-
pers, then hurriedly pulled on his cowboy boots. Cramming
his hat down on his head, he ran out to his truck. Loose
gravel spun out behind him as he gunned the accelerator and
rushed to Megan's.

As he drove, in spite of the rage, a sense of exhilarating
freedom rang through his soul. The moment he'd been
afraid of had come, and just as he'd prayed, his concern was
for Megan and Megan only. He didn't care what people said
about him, but she shouldn't be dragged through the mud
on his behalf. And he knew now, beyond a shadow of a
doubt, that he would give up his career in a heartbeat if it
would make things easier on her, as long as he thought it
was God's will.

When he pulled into her driveway, he forced himself to
slow down so she wouldn't be suspicious. He would stop out
at the front and pick up her papers, shove the one under the
seat and take the other to her. She'd think it was odd, him
being there so early, but hopefully she'd chalk it up to his
excitement at her decision.

He was happy with his plan until he saw the dewy grass
beside her mailbox. Empty. There were no newspapers

where they should have been, and that could only mean one thing. He yanked open the truck door and ran up to the house.

No longer caring what she thought about him being there, he banged on the door and called her name. "Megan."

There was no reply. He banged again. "Megan!"

After five minutes, a little voice answered. "Mr. Holt?"

"Yes, Sarah! Let me in. I have to see your mama." Instead of the expected unlocking of the door, there was nothing. Total silence. "Sarah?"

Finally, he heard her speak again. "She said to tell you to go away. She doesn't want you to come here anymore."

"Sarah, Honey, listen. Your mama needs me." Holt hated to try to convince the child to disobey her mother, but he knew Megan wasn't thinking clearly.

"She made me promise not to unlock the door. And I never break a promise." The last was said so proudly that Holt knew there was nothing more he could say.

"Okay, I'm going to go, but tell your mama I'm not giving up. Can you do that?"

"Uh-huh. I'll tell her."

He turned toward the truck.

"Mr. Holt?"

He spun around and put his mouth back to the door.

"Yes?"

"Mama threw up. She's sick, isn't she?"

"Maybe. But don't worry, Honey, she's going to be okay." He could only imagine how heartsick Megan must be.

"If she's sick, then we need to pray."

"You're right, Sarah, we do."

There was no more noise at the door, and Holt called Sarah's name a couple of times, but apparently, she'd gone back to be with her mother. He turned slowly and shuffled out to the truck, kicking every loose rock he could find.

When he pulled out of the driveway, he didn't turn toward his house. At first he wasn't sure why, then he saw the familiar red mailbox. Of course, he'd go talk to Aunt Irene. The elderly lady had known Megan a long time. If anyone could help him make her see reason, she could. In the meantime, he'd take Sarah's advice and pray.

≈

Sarah handed Megan a wet rag. Megan gazed into the worried face of her four year old and tried to smile. She knew she looked like a wreck. But unfortunately, even standing up was impossible right now. She still sat in the bathroom floor leaning against the vanity. When she first saw the picture, she'd been in the kitchen. She'd cried until she almost hyperventilated, then rushed to the bathroom to lose her breakfast. Sarah had apparently heard the noise and found her there.

Holt had come. She'd known he would. She'd tried to warn him about his persistence, but he refused to see the truth. Sarah had gone back and forth delivering messages, finally coming back with the last one. Holt would be praying for her.

When she heard that, for the first time since she saw the paper she thought of praying. Though she was still sure she had to give up Holt, peace covered her like a blanket when she was talking to God.

Funny how something like this made a person want their mama. She'd long ago alienated her mother, though, by constantly rebuffing her offers of help.

Megan wished it had been different, but surely her mother could see that pride wouldn't allow her to seek comfort from someone she'd inadvertently betrayed. Besides, this morning's paper had proven her right.

Anyone associated with Megan would be tainted by her past. Sarah slipped her small hand into Megan's and leaned against her.

Father, please give me strength to go on, for Sarah's sake. Help me to remember that You won't give me more than I can bear. I know that my suffering is nothing compared to what Jesus suffered on the cross or what You went through allowing Him to be put there. Forgive me for my weakness. Lord, be with Holt. Please keep him from harm and use him to do Your good work just as he desires for You to. In Jesus' name, amen.

Just as she finished praying, a knock sounded on the door again. She squeezed Sarah's hand. "Honey, would you please go tell Mr. Holt one more time to go away. Tell him I'm not going to change my mind." Sarah stood and started toward the door. "And Sarah? Whatever you do, don't let him in."

Though she couldn't make out the words, she knew Sarah was talking through the door, but suddenly she heard an unmistakable sound. Sarah had unlocked the door.

Megan bit back a cry and stumbled to her feet. A glance in the mirror confirmed she looked as bad as she felt.

Suddenly, her eyes fell on the heavy wooden bathroom door. She reached out and slammed it, throwing the slide lock into place just as she heard footsteps coming down the hall. A quick rap on the door sent her back to sit on the edge of the tub. One more knock. "Go away, Holt. I'm not coming out."

"Megan Marie! You open this door this instant."

Megan put her hand to her mouth. Her mother was here.

fifteen

"Holt, what are you doing here? Why, you brought my papers in. Thank you so much." Aunt Irene thumped in her big walking boot back over to the table and sat down in front of her still-steaming cup of coffee. "Come in and sit down. Tell me how the picnic went."

"The picnic was wonderful. Everyone loved Megan."

"Ah. . .runs in the family, huh?" Aunt Irene winked at him.

"Yeah, Megan and I decided last night to allow God to guide us in our relationship. She agreed to stop standing in the way."

The elderly woman clapped her hands together. "Oh, Holt. That's an answer to my prayers."

"Yeah, me too. Unfortunately, something happened this morning that complicates things."

A frown furrowed her brow. "What?"

"Hold onto your chair, Aunt Irene." He unfolded the newspaper in front of her. "It's not very pleasant."

Her eyes widened as she saw the picture, but she scanned the words, reading the article in silence. When she finished she shook her head. "Poor Ivo."

"Poor Ivo?" Holt stared at her. Had she lost her mind? "Are you talking about this reporter?"

"Yes, Dear, I am. I've been praying for him. I hoped he was doing better, but it looks like he's still hurting dreadfully."

"Maybe you'd better explain."

"Ivo Pletka was the grandson of my closest neighbors. He and Barry Watson were best friends all through high school

134

and college. It was actually through him that Barry met Megan. Megan was staying for awhile with her Granny Lola. Ivo and Barry were on a college break visiting Ivo's grandparents. Ivo adored his grandfather, and the feeling was mutual." He noticed Aunt Irene pronounced Ivo with a long E. Holt had read it as a long I. He thought it more fitting the way she said it because it sounded sort of like "evil."

"Anyway, once Barry set his cap for Megan, there was no stopping them. She was taken in by his smooth talk and handsome smile." She looked thoughtful. "Most everyone around was, including Ivo's grandparents."

"But not you?"

"No, every time I was around him, I just had this powerful feeling of being in the same room with a deadly snake."

"So he and Ivo were two of a kind, huh?"

She frowned again. "Not at all. Ivo was kind-hearted. He was just as awestruck as everyone else by his persuasive friend."

Holt tapped the paper. "So how did he get to this point?"

Tears welled up in Aunt Irene's eyes, and she surreptitiously brushed them away. "Ivo's grandfather was a Czechoslovakian immigrant. He'd had a hard life, and he was thrilled at the idea of being part of something that would help people have fun. Barry easily persuaded him to invest his life savings into the theme park he planned."

"So Ivo blames Megan for his grandfather losing money? Probably took a chunk out of his inheritance, huh?"

Aunt Irene reached over and patted his hand. She shook her head. "It wasn't the money. Ivo lost something far more than that. Two months after Barry's death, Mary Pletka had to put her husband in a nursing home. He'd totally lost his ability to take care of himself. He didn't even recognize Ivo anymore. Some said it was Alzheimer's. Others thought it was a stroke. But that boy knew in his heart that his grandfather's condition was due to misplaced trust."

"If he was that close to them, why couldn't he see that Megan had nothing to do with it?"

"When guilt crowds in on you, you want to dole it out to others. Ivo was free with his blame. He's estranged from his own grandmother. If he wasn't, he'd know. . ."

"Know what?"

Aunt Irene looked up at him as if surprised that she'd said that. "Bless her heart. She cries for him every time I see her."

"If he wasn't estranged from his grandmother, he'd know what?"

Aunt Irene dipped a generous spoonful of sugar from the jar on the table and placed it in her coffee. "I've got four pups that need to be fed right away. Think you can handle it?"

Exasperation coursed through him. "If I do, will you tell me what you were about to say?"

"I might. . .and I might not. I'll be talkin' to the Lord about it whilst you're feedin'."

Holt could see arguments would get him nowhere, so he hurried to perform the assigned task.

Ten minutes later, he stomped the dirt off his feet on the welcome mat and hurried in. Aunt Irene sat where he left her, coffee cup still in front of her, but she was smiling. "You going to go see Ivo?"

"Yes, Ma'am, I am. I have to stop him from persecuting Megan any further. If he doesn't, I'll take legal action."

She shook her head. "You won't stop him with threats, Boy."

He took a deep breath. "What will stop him?"

"The truth."

"And you have the truth?"

She drained the last of her coffee. "Yes, just so happens, I do."

"Then how come you haven't told Ivo?"

"I've given my solemn promise."

Holt wanted to let it go, but he knew he had to ask. "Then why are you about to tell me?"

"I never promised not to tell you. . .just him."

"Okay, I guess that makes sense. Was it Megan that you promised?"

"Do you enjoy playing Twenty Questions? Or would it be okay if I just tell you the whole thing?"

Holt had been staring at the table, trying to control his impatience, but her question brought his gaze quickly back to meet hers. Her blue eyes were faded, but a twinkle danced in them.

He took a deep breath and, in spite of the churning in his stomach, smiled at her spunk. "Why don't you just tell me?"

☙

Megan threw the lock back and yanked the door open. Her mother stood, tears streaming down her face, with her arms held out. With a great gulping sob, Megan fell into her embrace. "Oh, Mama. I'm so glad you came."

"I should have come three years ago, Child. I knew you needed me then, and every time I've seen you since then I've blamed myself for not being here for you."

"I. . . ," Megan shuddered and choked out the words. "I told you not to."

Her mother chuckled softly. "Don't you know by now that a mother isn't supposed to obey the daughter?"

Megan didn't answer but just relaxed against the woman whose arms she'd missed so badly. Even though she'd made sure Sarah spent time with her grandparents over the last three years, Megan had always had an excuse to keep from spending any time with them herself. Now, with the familiar smell of her mother's perfume soothing her wounded soul, she couldn't think why she'd behaved so stupidly.

Finally, she broke the embrace. "Where's Sarah?"

"She's out on the porch with your father."

"Daddy's here too?" Megan had been sure her father would be happy to have his only daughter fade quietly from his life after the scandal she'd brought to him. As a corporate lawyer, image was everything.

"Are you kidding? By the time I was dressed, he was in the car honking the horn. He's the one who saw the paper first, and he immediately called the office and told them to cancel his appointments because he was going to see his daughter."

"Oh, Mama, I'm so glad you did. Let's go sit down before my legs give out again, though." It almost seemed too much to take in all at once.

A few minutes later, Megan watched in amazement as her mother took charge and quickly made coffee and popped some cinnamon rolls in the oven. She hadn't even thought of the fact that this was where her mother had been raised. No wonder she seemed at home in the kitchen. Megan hadn't done any remodeling and Granny Lola hadn't either as long as Megan could remember. "Has the house changed much since you lived here?"

Megan's mother gave her a wry grin. "Not a bit. I didn't realize how much I missed this house, while I was giving my daughter 'her space' as my counselor called it."

"Oh, Mama. You had to get counseling because of me. I'm a terrible daughter."

"No, you're not. I needed advice on how to handle the situation with you. I wanted to shake you for your foolish pride and hug you for your determination all at the same time. But the counselor and I both agreed—if I crowded you, I'd lose you." She chuckled. "I didn't call to ask him what he thought about us coming today. I just went with a mother's instinct."

"It was right on target. I needed you."

"Are you ready to talk about the newspaper?"

Megan nodded. Running from her parents hadn't helped so far. "Will Dad mind getting it all secondhand? I'd rather Sarah not hear everything."

"Not at all. That's what we planned on the way here. He'd play with Sarah, while I talked to you. So, let's start with Senator McFadden. What does he mean to you?"

"I'm in love with him." Her mother started to smile, but it died on her lips when hot tears splashed down Megan's face. "But it'll never work. The newspaper is proof of that."

"Oh, Megan. Are you sure you're not doing again what you did with me? Pushing him away because of pride?"

"You knew that was the reason, huh?" Megan cast a sideways glance at her mom. "You're pretty smart."

"Yeah, well, I admit the counselor helped me figure that one out."

"Anyway, the answer is no. That's not what I'm doing with him. Holt is a Christian, Mama, and he believes that God has led him into a political career. He dreams of being governor of Arkansas someday and doing great things for God."

Her mother covered her mouth. Megan saw tears fill her eyes.

Megan nodded. "I see that you know I'm not just making a mountain out of a molehill. A relationship with me would be death to his career. I can't let that happen."

"Oh, Meggie. . .that's not for you to decide alone. I know it seems hopeless, but that's got to be partly his decision."

Megan shook her head emphatically. "No. He would give up his career for me, then he'd never be happy and even worse, he'd be going against what he believes God has in mind for him." She pushed her hair back from her face. "If I really love him—and I do—I can't let him do that."

"Well, you can't force someone to see things your way. Even your own daughter. So I won't try to argue with you. I'll just be here to support you." Her mother reached over to take her hand. "Of course that doesn't mean that I'm giving up on you finding happiness with Holt, if it's God's will."

Megan just shook her head. "And people wonder where I get my stubbornness."

sixteen

Aunt Irene smiled at Holt. "You want a cup of coffee to drink while I'm talkin'?"

"No, Ma'am," Holt clenched his hands and unclenched them. "Just go ahead and talk."

She shook her head. "Anybody ever tell you that you were impatient?"

Holt looked at the ceiling, then back at her. "I might have heard that once or twice."

"I bet you have."

"Aunt Irene, please." The pleading in his voice must have gotten through because she finally began.

"When Megan's husband died, she was mighty sorrowful. She had to deal with grief and betrayal all at once, plus there were all the investors to handle. It seemed more than she could bear. Her granny had been dead about six months when this all happened, or you can be sure that's where Megan would have run to. Instead, she showed up here. I like to think it was because she knew she could trust me, but I know it was partly 'cause I was one of the few in these parts that had refused to invest in Barry Watson's pipe dream. So she could face me."

Holt nodded. He could see Megan's pride keeping her from seeking help from anyone who had lost money in her husband's deal.

"We sat right here at this table, while little Sarah played on the floor, and we prayed and talked and prayed some more. After awhile, she asked me for a tablet and a pencil, and I got her one out of the drawer there." She nodded toward the kitchen drawer.

"She began to make a list. Every asset she had went down on that paper, along with the money she thought it was worth. She and Barry had a nice house in Jonesboro. They each had a late model car. One smart thing Barry had done—they were all paid for. As soon as she wrote down the house and the cars, she started listing her personal property—her jewelry and knickknacks and such. Then came the furniture. Finally, when she could think of nothing else to list, she stopped and totaled it all up."

Holt's gaze was glued to the old woman's expressive face. In spite of her simple speech, the word picture she painted was so vivid that he could almost see Megan seated at the table beside him, working feverishly on her list of assets. His heart ached for her all over again.

Aunt Irene's voice broke through his thoughts. "She tore off another page and pulled some papers out of her purse. She began to make another list. This one was people's names. All of the investors. Out beside their names was the amount of money they'd invested."

She shook her head. "She must have sat here for hours trying to balance those two lists. But even taking Barry's life insurance policy off the top, it couldn't be done. I'll never forget what she said. 'I have to pay the rest of it back, Aunt Irene. Somehow, God will help me find a way.' I asked her where she would live, and she offered me a pale smile. 'You don't mind a new neighbor, do you?' she asked. I told her nothing would make me happier."

"So she sold the house and all of her stuff and paid the investors what she could?" The thought of Megan going through that alone sent a physical pain through his stomach.

"Yep."

"But after her assets, including the life insurance policy, were depleted, there was nothing else she could do about that debt, right? And that's what keeps her hiding out? Pride?"

"Ah, we're back to playing quiz games, I see. Want me to just nod, or should I yell out 'hot' when you get close to the truth or 'cold' when you're farther away?"

In spite of his impatience, Holt couldn't bite back a grin. The elderly lady's dry wit had an edge that endeared her to him. "No, Ma'am, you just go ahead, and I'll try my best to keep quiet until you finish."

"All right, then." Aunt Irene tilted her coffee mug up and drained it. "Now where was I? Oh, yes, I remember. I went with Megan and Sarah down to Lola's house that day. You should have seen Megan's tired eyes light up when they saw that great big quilting machine. 'There it sits,' she said. 'The answer to my prayers.' And she was right."

Again the elderly lady swiped at tears. "Thankfully, Barry hadn't gotten as far in his scheme as he could have, so when he died there were only about twenty investors. Megan was able to pay off most of the smaller ones completely with their share of the life insurance policy and the sale of her assets. By the time everything was gone, she'd whittled the list of people who were still owed down to ten names."

Holt thought of Megan. She'd handled a horrible situation with grace and courage. Most people would have bowed under the load.

"She went into Batesville and took the money she'd gotten from selling her wedding ring. 'Seed money,' she called it. She bought two big rolls of quilt batting and all kinds of fabric. She put out flyers all over town."

He'd never thought of Megan as enterprising. But it sounded like she was. Then he remembered her sparsely furnished house and the fact that she wore the same clothes often and Sarah did too.

"It didn't really pay off for her, did it? She must barely make enough for her and Sarah to live."

Aunt Irene snorted. Holt realized he'd asked another question, and he held up his hands. "Forget I asked that. Just go on, please." She nodded.

"Yes, it wasn't long before all Lola's old customers as well as plenty of new ones were calling. She's stayed so busy quilting ever since, there's been little time for anything else. 'Til you came around, that is. Then she started making time."

Holt bit his lip to keep the questions from coming out.

"As soon as she took in money on her first quilt top, she took those ten names on that list and set up ten promissory notes, of sorts. Payments ranged from small to fairly large. That was three years ago."

Holt let the full meaning of what she was saying sink into his brain. "She's paying back all the investors."

"Well, congratulations, Holt! You win the game. That's exactly right. And Ivo Pletka would know that too, if he would talk to his grandma. But the boy's too stubborn. His grandfather had been in bad health for a long time, but his grandma had tried to protect Ivo by not telling him. Now, he won't believe her. He'd rather blame Barry, and since Barry's gone, in his eyes that leaves Megan to blame."

Holt put his head in his hands. He was going to confront the reporter that he'd so grudgingly prayed for this morning, but it wasn't going to be the confrontation he'd expected.

Instead, it looked like he was going to hit Ivo Pletka with the most powerful weapon of all. The truth.

An incredible thought flashed through his mind. Why would Pletka choose now to renew his persecution of Megan? Someone was behind this smear campaign. Someone who had already promised him he'd be sorry.

&

Megan wrapped her hands around the glass of iced tea. Her father sat next to her in the rocker, and her mother had taken Sarah in to make doll clothes.

"I've really messed things up for us, haven't I, Daddy?"

"Yes, Meg, you have."

Megan knew it was true, but her heart froze in her chest at his words. Her mother had seemed so sure that he was not upset with her.

"I'm sorry for not seeing Barry for what he really was."

"That's not how you messed things up for us, Megan. What you've done is allow your pride to keep us apart. We wanted to help you shoulder the load you've borne for the last three years, and you didn't let us." His deep voice was gentle, and love for his daughter was evident in his tone.

Tears poured down Megan's cheeks. "Daddy, I did it for you. For you and Mama. I knew what a scandal it was for y'all, but I hoped if I stayed away and didn't have contact with you, people would let you forget it."

"People?" He reached over and pushed her hair off her face. "What people do you think are more important than our only daughter?"

Megan looked at him, and sincerity was evident in his eyes. Had she misjudged things so badly? Was it possible that her parents had really wanted a close relationship with her even though she'd brought shame to them?

In some ways, it was harder to honor that desire than it had been just to stay away. She'd thought herself as strong these last three years, but she was starting to wonder if she'd taken the coward's way out instead.

❧

Holt slammed his truck door and strode across the paved circle-drive in front to the colonial mansion. A couple of calls on his cell phone had verified that Marshall was at home this morning, playing tennis with his daughter.

Going for an element of surprise, Holt bypassed the whole front door routine and slipped through the gate he knew was always unlocked. From afar, he stood for a second and watched the trim-looking older man lobbing the ball to the stunning brunette.

As he approached, he decided to give them fair warning. "Marshall," he called. "We need to talk."

Marshall Whitmore spun around, and the bright yellow ball bounced past him coming to a stop not far from Holt's feet.

Holt bent and scooped it up. Giving it a squeeze, he then began to toss it from hand to hand.

Marshall's eyes narrowed. "Talk? I thought you weren't able to talk to me? Something about me not being in your district?"

"What I'm here to talk about has nothing to do with my political opinions. This is personal."

Gloria started forward and as she got even with the net, Holt saw her paste a sweet smile on as if it were a postage stamp. Why hadn't he ever noticed her phoniness before?

"Personal?" Her voice was squeaky with anticipation. Apparently, she hadn't replaced him yet, in spite of her dislike for his "hick" ways.

"Yes, personal with your father." She gave a practiced pout, and he realized he had some unfinished business with her, as well. "On second thought you can stay."

"Holt, have you come to your senses?" asked Marshall Whitmore.

"Yes, Marshall, as a matter of fact, I have." Holt continued to toss the ball up and catch it.

"Well, good, I'm glad to hear that." Marshall lowered the racket he'd been holding almost defensively and nodded. "Come on in, and let's have some coffee. I'll tell you what we need to do."

"No, I'm afraid that's not going to work. Because I've come to tell you what we're going to do. Or rather what you're going to do." Holt silently thanked God for his total lack of fear. After years of praying "Your will be done," he was finally living it as far as his career was concerned.

Marshall sputtered. "What do you mean?"

"I mean this. You are going to leave me alone. You're going to leave Megan Watson alone. You aren't ever going to pay anyone to follow us again. As a matter of fact, you're going to forget we ever existed. Do you know why you're going to do this?"

"I don't—" Marshall's face was as red as the brick on the house in the distance.

"Don't even think about denying what you've done." Holt squeezed the tennis ball with one hand. "We're beyond that. Now we're going to talk about the future. If you don't forget about us, I'll be forced to bring allegations against you for trying to force me to vote your way on important issues. I'm giving you a chance to turn over a new leaf."

Marshall was turning redder by the second. "Get off—"

"As you can tell, I'm no longer following the things you taught me, back when you were 'grooming' me to become governor. No, you always said, 'Never give an enemy a second chance.'" Holt gave the ball one more hard squeeze. "If you were me, you'd go straight to a reporter with these charges, wouldn't you?"

When Holt said the word reporter, the redness drained from Marshall's face like a broken thermometer. He worked his mouth but nothing came out.

"Let me just tell you like it is. I was elected to represent the people and vote their wishes. As long as their wishes don't violate my conscience, I intend to do just that." Holt had always thought politicians were supposed to take care not to be too firm in their stances. After all, fanaticism bred contempt more than familiarity ever had.

The man standing in front of him had taught him that. But Holt found himself unable, and unwilling, to stand behind the invisible fence anymore.

"With all due respect," Holt said, praying for the right words, "you told me once that money talks. Well, God talks too. And He says you can only serve one master, Him or money." He cleared his throat and plunged on. "God put me where I am today, not you. And whether you choose Him or not, I do."

Marshall didn't say anything. Holt turned to Gloria who stood slack-jawed, staring. "Gloria, before I go I'm going to do you a favor, as well. You need to get a life. First, you need to learn what love really is, then you need to find someone with whom you can share it. Real love—the kind that can only come from knowing God—isn't about political influence. Don't marry some 'hick' because your daddy tells you to."

He was surprised to see tears in her eyes. She didn't speak but only nodded.

He tossed the tennis ball to Marshall, who stood dumbly and let it bounce by. With a nod, Holt turned and retraced his steps. Two down, one to go.

seventeen

Catching her mother in the kitchen and her father playing with Sarah, Megan slipped away to her room. She locked the door quietly and sank down on her bed. Her head was spinning from the things her father had said. Was he right? Had her life been governed by foolish pride?

Oh, God, please don't let me make the same mistake again. Give me courage and strength. And, Lord, please give me wisdom. Tears burned a path down her cheeks. *Father, I'm so sorry. I've tried to handle everything alone, and I can see the pain that has caused my earthly father. I can only imagine how much more my pride has hurt You, who could have handled my problems so easily.*

I should have confronted Ivo three years ago and trusted You to make him believe me. But I was afraid. And, deep down, I guess I wanted to prove him wrong instead of just telling him he was wrong about me. That was pride, wasn't it? A wracking sob shook her body. *What a mess I've made. Please forgive me. Through Jesus I pray, amen.*

She rose slowly to her feet and hurried into the bathroom to wash her face. It was never too late to change. That's what her parents had taught her from the time she was tiny, and God's Word taught the same thing. It was time she acted on that.

She hurried to the closet and scanned the few outfits that hung there. Finally settling on one that had been her favorite three years before, she pulled it out and laid it on the bed.

She was tired of being a coward. How had she forgotten the boy David? He'd understood that it didn't matter how big the giant was, but only how big God was.

❧

When Megan walked out onto the porch, her mother saw her first and jumped to her feet.

"Megan!"

Her father swung around from where he was squatted down playing dolls with Sarah on the wood planks. He lost his balance and sat down hard on his seat. A broad grin creased his face. "Knocked me clean off my feet, Girl."

"Why are you all dressed up, Mama?" Sarah scampered over to her mother's side and reached out a tentative hand to the pale blue silk suit Megan was wearing. "Your eyes look as blue as the sky."

"Thanks." She smiled gently at her daughter and glanced up to meet her mother's gaze. "Can you all stay with Sarah for awhile?"

Megan watched in amusement as her mother gave her father "The Look." That particular expression had a variety of meanings. Megan knew years of marriage told her father that right now it meant, "Take Sarah to play so I can talk to Megan."

When he nodded, her mother rewarded him with a look that plainly said, "I'll tell you all about it later."

Megan suppressed a giggle as she thought of how many wordless conversations she'd witnessed between her parents over the years. Would she ever have that kind of easy communication with anyone? She thought of all the comfortable silences she'd shared with Holt.

As soon as her father and Sarah were walking across the yard, Megan's mother turned to her. "Where are you going?"

"I'm just going to take care of some things I should have done years ago."

"You look beautiful." Tears filled her mother's eyes. "I'd despaired of ever seeing you like this again."

"Dressed up?"

"No. At peace."

The two women embraced. Megan could feel her makeup start to run. She pulled back, swiping her damp cheeks with the back of her hand, and giving a few rapid blinks to scare the offending tears away. "I'm not sure when I'll be home. I have my cell phone. Call me if you need me."

"We'll be fine. You've done a good job of raising Sarah. She's a pleasure to be around."

Megan nodded. The words eased another brick of guilt off her heart. Maybe she hadn't warped Sarah permanently by forcing her own self-imposed exile on her daughter.

"Thanks, Mom." She stepped into the house long enough to get her purse and keys, then she ran out to hug Sarah good-bye.

"Mr. Holt told me a story once, and we pretended you were a beautiful princess locked in a tower. I think you really are."

Megan laughed. "Oh, he did, did he? Well, this princess is busting out."

Sarah turned to the section of grass beside her. "Lucy, do you know what she means?"

Megan kissed her on the forehead and offered an air-kiss to the invisible Lucy. "I'll explain it later, Baby. I've got to run."

She hurried to the van, and even though she wasn't used to the high heels, it felt like her feet were barely touching the ground.

So, Holt was right. . .freedom really is a state of mind.

❧

Holt walked down the corridor formed by the gray tweed walls of cubicles. When he'd almost reached the right one, the sound of raised voices told him his target wasn't alone.

He spied a plastic chair sitting next to the water cooler nearby and sank down in it to wait his turn. In spite of the buzz of office noise, much of the conversation was easy to hear.

"It took you long enough to come out of hiding. That in itself tells me you are guilty." Anger laced the male voice.

"You're the one who. . ." The woman's voice was somewhat softer, and Holt couldn't completely make out either her words or her tone.

He glanced at a small corkboard covered with cartoons, fastened by everything ranging from an actual thumbtack to a toothpick. Despite trying to concentrate on the funnies instead of eavesdropping, he couldn't miss the man's words. They were barely short of a shout.

"My grandfather trusted you. And you betrayed him." From his vantage point, Holt saw a couple of people poke their heads out of their cubicles and cast curious glances toward the direction of the heated words.

The softer voice sounded soothing at first, then it too rose in unmistakable anger, and Holt gasped. It couldn't be. . .

"I didn't have anything to do with it! I was betrayed just as you were. I would have done anything to make it right again, but you didn't even come and ask me about it. In spite of our friendship, you assumed I was guilty, and you used your power as a reporter to make sure others thought it too. I've suffered for three years, thinking somehow I deserved it. . ." The familiar voice softened again, "But I didn't. I didn't deserve it anymore than you deserved what happened to your grandfather. I'm sorry, Ivo."

"That's easy for you to say now. But can you prove to me you had nothing to do with it?" Holt got to his feet, ready to defend. But beneath the blustery anger Holt could hear the hope in the man's voice, the desire to know that only one of his friends had betrayed him.

"I. . ." Megan stopped short, and Holt knew that in spite of her new attitude, she would never tell Pletka the one thing that would convince him.

He stepped to the door of the cubicle. "I can."

Megan's face went as white as her blouse.

The red-haired man spun around. "Who are you?"

"You mean you don't recognize me from your latest smear campaign? I'm Senator Holt McFadden."

Pletka sank down in his chair. "What do you want?" he sneered.

"You asked for proof of Megan's innocence. I happen to have it. And 'what do I want?' you ask? I want a retraction and an apology."

"I'm not apologizing to you. If you couldn't stand the heat, you should have stayed out of politics."

"I don't want an apology for me. I want one for Megan."

"Oh." Ivo seemed to deflate before their eyes. He rubbed his eyes and ran his finger through his already disheveled hair. "Where's your proof?"

"Call your grandmother. That's my proof."

Megan gasped. "How could you know that?" she whispered.

Holt stared at her, taking in every detail of her elegant upswept hairdo and silk suit, right down to the strappy high-heeled sandals. She was pure class. But then she always had been. Even on the farm. He just hoped she could forgive him for butting in.

"Know what?" Pletka sat up straight again, his reporter's instincts kicking back in. "What do you know? And what does calling my *babicka* have to do with anything?"

"She can verify what I'm going to tell you." Holt was surprised at the twinge of sympathy he felt for the mixed-up young man before him. Another look at Megan's white face sent the newly found pity scurrying to the back of his heart.

"Holt. . ." Megan's voice was trembling.

"If you really don't want me to, I won't."

"Would somebody please tell me what you're talking about?" The bluster was back full force in the reporter's voice.

"Go ahead," Megan said with a nod.

Holt turned to Pletka. "When Barry died, Megan sold everything they had and moved to her grandmother's farm house. She also took over the quilting business."

Ivo snorted. "Tell me something I don't know."

"Okay, I will. She took the money she had from the sale and divided it equally among the twenty investors. Ten of them were paid off at that time, with interest. But ten remained. The remaining ten have been receiving monthly payments from Megan for the last three years. She's scrimped and pinched pennies, until a man about town like you would be ashamed to know the amount of money she's been raising her little girl on. By doing that, she's almost succeeded in paying back every penny people lost in Barry's investment, plus interest."

Pletka's ruddy complexion paled, his freckles standing out like blots of rusty ink on a sheet of white paper. He shook his head. "I can't. . . Oh. . . That's not. . ." He put his head in his hands and sobs wracked his body.

Megan had stood frozen in place while Holt talked but she suddenly bolted forward. She stood behind Ivo and patted him gently on the back. "Ivo, your grandmother would love to hear from you. She prays every night that you'll call."

He jerked his head up and turned to look at Megan. "She defended you, and I couldn't stand it. I had to have someone to blame. Barry was dead, so I blamed you. She even tried to tell me later. I know now she was trying to make me see you were paying the money back, but I wouldn't listen." The words poured out of him like an unstopped fountain. "These past few months, I've been going to a church here in town, and I've been thinking a lot about forgiveness, but then. . ." He stopped and looked at Holt.

"Then Marshall Whitmore approached you about doing another story. Provided you with a picture that looked incriminating and made you think you were doing a service for your country by keeping Megan from corrupting an elected official."

Ivo nodded, his eyes brimming with tears. He looked from Holt to Megan. "I'm so sorry. Can you ever forgive me?"

Megan nodded. "I'm hoping forgiveness is the order of the day." She looked at Holt, and hope leaped in his stomach. Then she turned back to Ivo. "I should have confronted you a long time ago, and we could have avoided all of this." She squeezed Ivo's shoulder. "You going to be all right?"

He nodded and patted her hand. "I'm going to call my *babicka*."

"Good." Her smile encompassed Holt, as well, and the crazy events of the day just all seemed to melt away. "I'd better go. I left Sarah at the farm with Mom and Dad."

Holt raised an eyebrow. "Your parents are at the farm?"

Megan nodded, and Holt could see the true peace in her eyes.

"I'll walk you out," Holt said.

"Wait." Ivo stood and lightly embraced Megan. "Senator McFadden, would you mind staying for awhile? I have some things I'd like to talk to you about."

Disappointment covered Holt like a moldy blanket. What could he say? Yes, he minded terribly because he couldn't wait another minute to be alone with Megan? "No. . .uh. . . that's fine."

A small smile teased at Megan's mouth, and a dimple flashed so quickly he wasn't sure his imagination hadn't played tricks on him. It was almost as if she could read his thoughts. She gave a little wave and stepped out into the corridor.

"See you at the farm later," he called.

She nodded without looking back. Holt stood in the doorway and watched her glide away, swinging her tiny purse as she walked, until she disappeared from sight. He was tired of these constant good-byes.

eighteen

Holt sped down Megan's driveway and came to a stop beside a shiny silver sedan. He grimaced.

Patience, Lord. Please.

The familiar prayer brought a half-smile to his lips. He was convinced God had brought Megan into his life. But maybe it was his own prayers that had persuaded God to introduce him to Megan. After all, he seemed to be practicing his patience every day since he'd met her.

The whole drive from Little Rock, he'd thought of nothing but holding Megan in his arms and declaring his feelings to her. He'd expected to have to distract Sarah first, but her parents? Obviously, those plans would have to wait. In spite of his impatience, he had to admit he was thankful she was working things out with her parents.

He got out of the truck, and before he could get halfway up the path to the house, Sarah catapulted into his arms. He grinned as he hoisted her onto his shoulders and carried her the rest of the way. When they reached the porch, he swung her to the ground, laughing aloud at her squeals of delight.

"Looks like you've got you a buddy there."

Holt swung around. A distinguished-looking gentleman about twenty-five years Holt's senior sat in one of the rockers. "Yes, Sir. We're good friends, aren't we, Sarah?"

"Uh-huh." She studied Holt for a minute. "Most of my friends are 'may-nay' but you're not."

Holt pinched himself. "Ouch." He shook his head. "No, I guess I'm real."

Sarah giggled.

The man in the rocker smiled. "You must be Holt. I'm Ransom Jackson, Megan's dad." He stuck out his hand.

Holt shook the offered hand. "It's nice to meet you."

"You too. I've heard a lot about you."

Holt grinned.

"From Sarah. . ."

Holt's grin faltered.

"And Megan too, of course."

Holt looked at the teasing glint in Ransom Jackson's eyes and knew, he was going to get along just fine with Megan's father.

❧

Later that evening, Megan stood beside Holt in the yard and watched her parents drive away. Even though she'd loved having them, she'd been waiting all evening for them to go. Megan's mother had insisted on reading Sarah a bedtime story and tucking her in before they left.

"I really like them." Holt's voice sounded loud in the still night.

"Me too, but I thought they'd never leave." She giggled.

He reached over with one arm and drew her up against his side. "I know what you mean."

"Holt. . ." Her gut twisted, but she knew it had to be said. "Although we worked things out with Ivo, I'm still not sure it's the best idea for us to get involved."

Even in the moonlight, she could see the astonishment on his features. "Involved?" His chuckle was mirthless. "Is that what you call this? I think about you constantly. I want to be with you all the time. I'm so in love with you I can't think straight."

"Uh. . .that's kind of my point." She turned to face him, and he kept his arms at her waist. With one hand, she reached up and caressed his face. "You can't think straight. That's why I have to. God put you where you are."

"Yes, Ma'am, I agree. God put me where I am. In your arms."

She shook her head. "You know that's not what I meant. I mean God put you in the senate, with a desire in your heart to be governor."

"Now how did you know that?"

"I read between the lines."

"You think you're so smart." He started to tickle her, but when she spoke, his hands froze.

"I think we need to wait awhile."

"Wait awhile?"

"Yes. Let's wait and see how things settle down after Ivo prints his retraction. See if any other reporter is going to take up where he left off. Let's give ourselves some time and pray about our relationship. If it's meant to be, God will work it out."

"How do you know He hasn't already worked it out?"

"I don't know, but a little time isn't going to hurt anything." Was that really her voice saying those crazy things? A little time? Any amount of time away from him seemed like more than she could bear.

He stared down at her, and she watched the shadows play across his face. "Have it your way." She cringed at his obvious irritation. He leaned forward and whispered in her ear, his warm breath sending tingles up and down her spine. "You're definitely worth waiting for."

When he drew back, his mouth was inches from hers. He used his thumb to wipe away a tear she hadn't even realized she'd shed. He gently lowered his lips to hers. The chirping crickets faded away, and the sweet taste of promise sang through her soul. He drew back and dropped a light kiss on her forehead. "I'll try to be patient, but don't forget me."

She touched her lips, still warm from his kiss and shook her head, tears flowing in hot streams down her cheeks. Before he could say anything, she turned and ran into the house. She refused to watch him leave even one more time.

❧

"Why don't you just call him?" Aunt Irene asked.

Megan shook her head and continued to freehand stitch around the baskets. "I can't."

"Yes, you can. You've got a perfectly good telephone over there, and as far as I know, your hand's not broke."

Megan stopped the machine for a second and cast her gaze heavenward. "You know what I mean. This is probably for the best. I'm not a hermit anymore, but I still was associated with scandal. That's not the best person for an aspiring politician to mar—Er, to become involved with, I mean."

"Go ahead and say it. Marry. Cause you know, and I do too, it's what you want. You've got it bad, Child. All your quilts have got tearstains on them. And I thought you were through being a martyr."

"Aunt Irene, I'm not being a martyr. I'm being a realist, but in the meantime, I'm praying. So far, I've yet to see a way not to be a hindrance to Holt's career. If I figure it out, you'll be the first to know."

"No, Missy, I'll settle for second to know. You put that senator out of his misery first."

Megan glanced up from her quilting. "Just pray."

"I already am."

❧

One week later, Holt stared in the mirror. The man in there was barely recognizable. He couldn't sleep. He couldn't eat.

Lord, please, if it's not Your will for me to be with Megan for the rest of my life, to take her as my wife, then take this desire of my heart away and give me peace in its place or at least acceptance. Please, Father.

Without God's help, he couldn't accept it. They'd come so far. Overcome so many obstacles. Only to foul out in the bottom of the ninth with two outs and the bases loaded? Could it be this was God's will?

He stumbled from the bathroom and walked numbly through the house. The coffeepot gurgled happily, and Holt stopped long enough to pour himself some coffee. He'd forego the cream and sugar. Black suited his mood today.

He set the mug of coffee on the porch railing and walked out to get the newspaper. The action was so reminiscent of the day he'd walked out to get the papers only to have his world crash down around his ears that he shivered.

Both papers lay on the ground, and Holt just stared at them for a minute. Finally, he scooped them up and carried them back to the porch. Would Pletka's retraction be in today's paper? How many people would read a little correction? Ten percent of those who read the original story? Twenty?

He flipped open the free paper, and his mouth dropped open. The front page had a huge picture of Megan with Sarah.

WATSON'S WIDOW SACRIFICES TO REPAY HIS DEBTS

The headline was extra-large font. As Holt hungrily read the story, he realized Pletka had used everything he'd told him that day at the newspaper office and much, much more. He'd interviewed most of the investors, and they'd all told in their own words how much Megan's actions meant to them.

When he'd finished, he hugged the article to his chest and tossed the statewide paper to the side, then did a double take as it fell open. The same article, with the picture and headline slightly smaller was on the front page of this one, as well.

Holt's hands trembled. Full realization dawned on him. All of Megan's fears were laid to rest. There was nothing standing in the way. He fell to his knees on the board porch right there in the morning light.

Thank you, Lord. Thank you for hearing my prayer about Ivo Pletka and giving him a contrite heart. You truly are my rock and my fortress and my deliverer. Without You, I am nothing. You are worthy to be praised, Lord, and my faith lies completely in You.

When he finished, he rose and went into the house and showered, shaved, and dressed. With the newspapers tucked under his arm, he hurried to the truck and sped away.

nineteen

Megan breathed in the scent of roses. She smiled at Holt who sat next to her on an elegant, but amazingly comfortable, park bench. Water sparkled like diamonds in a beautiful fountain nearby. The brilliant green of the budding trees framed out the magnificent garden. She leaned against Holt, contentment filling her soul.

Suddenly, a small squirrel with a hammer popped out of the tree nearest Megan and began banging on the park bench they were sitting on. She jumped up and tried to grab him, but he dodged her attempts and continued to bang.

She squinted one eye open, then the other. No park. No park bench, comfortable or otherwise. So, why was the squirrel still here? She sat straight up. It was someone at the door. . .someone very persistent. As soon as she thought that word, she knew who it was. She leapt to her feet, slipped into her fuzzy houseshoes, and grabbed her pink terry cloth robe. Her pajamas were totally decent, but her mama had always taught her that a lady wore a robe when a gentleman was present.

Of course gentlemen don't bang on doors like a psychotic squirrel with a hammer either, she thought, cinching the belt and hurrying down the hallway. His mama must not have taught him that.

She threw open the door, and Holt picked her up and spun her around. As the room tilted and twirled, Megan held on for dear life. "Have you lost your mind?" she finally yelled.

He laughed and set her down on her feet with a thud. "I'm

crazy about you. Does that count?"

"Holt, I thought we were going to wait."

"That's right, and wait we did. But guess what? The waiting is over." He spread open two newspapers on the coffee table.

Megan stared at her picture in shocked silence for a second, then slowly reached to pick up a paper. As she read, great gulping sobs shook her shoulders. Holt moved over and put his arm around her.

"Mama! Why are you crying?"

Megan grinned at Sarah, but she was still sobbing too hard to speak. She looked at Holt and cried harder because she could see he knew instantly she wanted him to explain.

He released Megan and squatted down to hold Sarah. "It's something kind of strange that women do sometimes. Even you will someday." At Holt's idea of an explanation, Megan tried to frown at him. But like one of those little collapsible puppets, her tearful grin popped right back into place. "She's crying because she's happy, Honey."

Sarah looked doubtful. "I guess you're right 'cause I don't smile when I'm crying and neither does Lucy, but Mama sure is."

Megan nodded. Her sobs had subsided to a shuddering hiccupy one every once in awhile, so she bent down to hug Sarah. "I'm okay, Sweetie."

Sarah quickly lost interest and ran back to her room to play.

For an awkward moment, neither Megan nor Holt seemed to know what to say. Megan had worn the mantle of bondage so long that this unfamiliar cloak of freedom made her feel almost undressed.

"Stay right there. I have something for you." She turned and ran down the hall into the sewing room. She grabbed the red, white, and blue lap quilt. As she spun to hurry back, she paused for a second to survey the room that had been her haven for three years. She wouldn't have to give up her quilting business, but if she and Holt—assuming that's what he had in mind—attempted a future together, she would probably have to give up this room, where she'd felt so safe and secure.

Trading this room, no matter how warm and cozy, for the security of Holt's love reminded her of trading this life for the security of heaven. There was no comparison. She turned out the light and hurried down the hall.

❧

As Holt waited for Megan to come back, he couldn't keep from tapping his toe lightly on the floor.

When she came down the hall with something in her hands, she stopped. "Don't tell me."

"Don't tell you what?" he asked.

"That you're a toe-tapper." She tilted her head and examined his demeanor. "You are, aren't you?"

He started to deny it, but he knew it was true. "Yes, I am."

"I'm going to have to work on your problem with impatience." She grinned saucily.

He shook his head. "Believe me, you already have. More than you know."

She walked toward him again, and when she grew near, she leaned up to whisper in his ear. "Anything worth having is worth waiting for."

"Waiting for you has been an adventure I wouldn't have given up for anything, Meg." He leaned toward her, but she stepped back.

"Well, since I've taught you a thing or two about patience, it's only fair to admit that you've taught me something too."

"About persistence?"

She grimaced. "We won't even discuss that. About freedom. It really is a state of mind." She unfolded the lap quilt in her hands and held it up for him to see. "This is to keep you warm on those cold winter nights."

He stared at the beautiful flag quilt, obviously intended to commemorate his love for America. "Megan, it's beautiful. Did you make it?"

"Yes, Sir. With my own two hands. . .and my sewing machine and quilting machine."

He took it in his hands and admired the work, neat and precise like everything else about her. The caring that had gone into the simple blanket was almost tangible. "I love it. Thank you."

"You're welcome."

"I have to admit I'm a little disappointed, though."

She glanced up at him quickly. "You are? Oh, no. I knew better than to give a man a quilt, but I thought. . ."

He reached out his finger and placed it gently on her lips. "Shh. . ."

"But I. . ."

He took her in his arms and pulled her closer, smashing the quilt between them. "I'm disappointed because I was hoping by winter I would have something else to keep me warm during those cold nights."

Her eyes widened with understanding, and he thought he might drown in their crystal blue depths. He gently caressed her cheek with his thumb. "Megan. . ." He stepped back and carefully placed the quilt across the back of a chair. Then he took her hand and lowered himself to one knee on the hardwood floor. "Would you make me the happiest man in the world and agree to be my wife?"

Tears flowed down her cheeks. "On one condition."

He stood and took her in his arms. "What's that?"

"That you throw your patience out the window when it comes to setting a wedding date." She threw her arms around him. "I've had all the waiting I want."

He laughed. "I agree. Let's ask our little flower girl how soon she can be ready and go from there."

ىد

Megan knew Holt was right. They'd have to give Sarah time to adjust to such a big change. She had a horrifying vision of Sarah crying and refusing to share her mother with anyone. Sure, the little girl liked Holt, but she'd had her mama's undivided attention for so long. "When do you think we should tell her?"

"Well, since—thanks to your 'one condition'—my patience is currently residing out the window, I'd say now." He squeezed Megan's hand. "However she reacts, with God's help we can deal with it together."

Megan nodded, silently praying already. "Sarah," she called.

Seconds later, Sarah skipped into the room, her long blonde ponytail bobbing behind her. "Yes, Ma'am?"

"I need to talk to you."

"Mama, has Mr. Holt been making you happy again?" she asked sternly, nodding at the tears on Megan's cheeks.

"Actually, yes, he has." Megan sank down on the couch and pulled Sarah up on her lap, then nodded for Holt to sit too. When they were all settled, she continued. "You know your daddy died when you were a baby?"

Sarah nodded.

"We've made it fine by ourselves since then, but sometimes it's a little lonely, isn't it?"

Sarah shook her head. "Not anymore. Not since I have my

'may-nay' friends and you have Mr. Holt."

Megan glanced over Sarah's head at Holt. He offered a reassuring grin. "Yes, well, that's sort of what I wanted to talk to you about. Mr. Holt has asked me to marry him."

"Really?"

"Yes, really."

"Would he live with us like they do on TV when they get married?" Sarah's brow was furrowed.

"Yes, Honey, or we would live with him. We haven't worked that part out yet, but we would all live together as a family."

"And you'd have a wedding?"

"Yes, and we thought you might want to be a flower girl."

"When would the wedding be?"

Megan sighed, grateful that Sarah hadn't balked. . .yet.

"Well, we thought we might leave that up to you. If you'd like for us to take some time so you can get used to Mr. Holt. . ."

Sarah slid down off Megan's lap and ran over to Holt. She put her little hands on the side of his face. "When you marry my mommy, will you be my daddy?"

He nodded.

"Can we have the wedding today?"

Through her own blurred vision, Megan saw suspicious moisture in Holt's eyes. Neither of them could speak.

"Can Lucy be a flowery girl too? Will there be lots of people there? Will we have chocolate cake? Can Grandma—" Sarah's seemingly endless stream of questions was cut off as Holt stood and scooped her up into his arms. As her giggles filled the air, Megan rose and joined the embrace. Their gaze met above the small blond head.

"Ouch! You're squishing me." Sarah wriggled to the floor.

"I've got to go tell Lucy we're going to be flowery girls." She scampered down the hall.

Megan relaxed in Holt's arms, with her head against his chest. The steady beating of his heart reminded her so much of his personality. Constant and true. "I have a confession," she murmured.

He tilted her head up to face him. "Let's hear it."

"I'm thankful for your persistence."

"Aha! I knew it."

She reached up and brushed his lips with hers. As she started to pull back, he wrapped his arms around her more tightly. She surrendered to the sweet promise of his kiss and realized she'd found true freedom at last.

A Letter To Our Readers

Dear Reader:

In order that we might better contribute to your reading enjoyment, we would appreciate your taking a few minutes to respond to the following questions. We welcome your comments and read each form and letter we receive. When completed, please return to the following:

Fiction Editor
Heartsong Presents
PO Box 719
Uhrichsville, Ohio 44683

1. Did you enjoy reading *Patchwork and Politics* by Christine Lynxwiler?
   ❏ Very much! I would like to see more books by this author!
   ❏ Moderately. I would have enjoyed it more if

   _____

   _____

   _____

2. Are you a member of **Heartsong Presents**? ❏ Yes ❏ No
   If no, where did you purchase this book? _____

   _____

3. How would you rate, on a scale from 1 (poor) to 5 (superior), the cover design? _____

4. On a scale from 1 (poor) to 10 (superior), please rate the following elements.

   ___ Heroine   ___ Plot
   ___ Hero   ___ Inspirational theme
   ___ Setting   ___ Secondary characters

5. These characters were special because?_____

_____

_____

6. How has this book inspired your life?_____

_____

_____

7. What settings would you like to see covered in future
   Heartsong Presents books? _____

_____

_____

8. What are some inspirational themes you would like to see
   treated in future books? _____

_____

_____

9. Would you be interested in reading other **Heartsong
   Presents** titles? ❏ Yes   ❏ No

10. Please check your age range:
    ❏ Under 18   ❏ 18-24
    ❏ 25-34   ❏ 35-45
    ❏ 46-55   ❏ Over 55

Name_____

Occupation _____

Address _____

City_____ State_____ Zip_____

MISSOURI GATEWAYS

*F*rom the land of the Gateway Arch to the City of Fountains, stirring romances occur in the bookend cities of Missouri. But when it appears, will these four young, professional, African-American women have the faith to believe in the real thing?

Contemporary, paperback, 464 pages, 5 ³/₁₆" x 8"

❤ ❤ ❤ ❤ ❤ ❤ ❤ ❤ ❤ ❤ ❤ ❤ ❤ ❤ ❤ ❤

❤ ❤ ❤ ❤ ❤ ❤ ❤ ❤ ❤ ❤ ❤ ❤ ❤ ❤ ❤ ❤

Presents